Jean-François Kouadio

THE REPUBLIC
OF MONKEYS

This book was first published by Botsotso in 2018

Box 30952
Braamfontein
2017
South Africa

Email: botsotso@artslink.co.za
www.botsotso.org.za

ISBN: 978-0-9947081-1-3

Editor: Allan Kolski Horwitz

For my lifetime friends, Gecille Hindson & Franklin H. White

Sincere acknowledgements also to:

Dr. James Ocita
Warren J. Trokis
Diane Howerton
Allan Kolski Horwitz
Tejumabe A. Oke
Palesa Mazamisa
Bruno A. Kouassi
Michaël F. Yéré
Allouan Kouamé
Guillaume W. Kouamé
Charles N. N'goran
Diomandé Sekou
Guy Gérard Aloco

FOREWORD

The Republic of Monkeys, as a title, will impress Africa's colonial masters immensely as what it presents clearly shows the near complete failure of the Black African state – as predicted by the imperialists at the onset of the independence movement.

The publishers *Faber and Faber* of London, in accepting Peter Abraham's *A Wreath of Udomo,* praised the 'half-caste' author for giving them a dispassionate book without the bitterness or self-pity that obscures African writing. "Here, thank goodness, is a book that is not about race in which there are good whites and bad blacks…" so goes the blurb. The realists, African or other, may even praise the title depending on which side of Kouadio's politics they fall. The author paints for us African rulers as not much above clever apes in the impenetrable jungles of State Houses insofar as their treatment of those they rule reveals their true colours. Having said this, the work does not attempt nor pretend to prescribe antidotes to the intrigues, lies, betrayals, treacheries, brutalities, coup d'états and skulduggeries that continue to bedevil African centres of state power.

The genre of the work is fiction delivered as short stories equally readable under a single theme. But it is easy for one to think of it as an account of the politics of present day Ivory Coast, where most of the action takes place. The style greatly suggests French influence; the humour, severity and even serenity are certainly French oriented – reminiscent of Guy de Maupassant and Gustave Flaubert but combined! The theme is African politics at work, replete with the usual accompaniment of religious pastors and their chanting, lamb-like flocks. The author highlights the spurious, albeit utterly powerful, influence of religious cults and the occult, witchcraft and religious mumbo jumbo which is exhaustively and successfully used by African head of states.

The collection is also a steadfast comment on African values and social issues like the horror of female genital mutilation, environmental degradation and the limitless greed for power – all evils which are roundly blamed as hindrances to progress. In addition, Kouadio travels beyond fiction and delves into the field of political economy. He depicts the scourge of poverty in African cities and how the politicians, the pastors and the hardened 'expert' city dwellers exploit this depravity to manipulate the masses for their own survival in this dog-eat-dog situation. It is through his juxtaposition of characters in the areas of politics and religion, ethno-tribalism and regionalism, that we take a broad look at Ivory Coast, at East Africa, indeed, at Africa herself, and at our individual selves so that we both laugh and weep – and in this work we get laughter and tears in equal measure.

The plots are centred on diverse characters (most of whom are top politicians, army officers, corrupt policemen, fanatical religious personalities) and, to some extent, their families. We don't find heroes or heroines but evil men galore whose conniving is generally practiced against the masses. But the chief protagonists don't meet to wrench out their own guts or anger in physical struggle. Their armies and police (with their deadly paraphernalia of tools) along with marauding rebels are manipulated to quench the blood-lust of these 'big men' by bludgeoning demonstrators at rallies and religious gatherings and hacking human beings in remote trading centres. It is in the ghastly raw matter and gory twitching of the amputated body parts of the lamblike flock that we witness the true state of anarchy and brutality in the aftermaths of political upheavals; when radio stations belch out impossible to believe coup d'état's and generals-cum-presidents arrive in European capitals on jetliners without regretting the plight of those they 'led astray' (and marooned) in the fight to fill their individual stomachs.

The Republic of Monkeys is very readable, its flow running naturally from the first pages. I believe it to be one of the best fiction works of today.

Lieutenant-Colonel Ulysses Chuka Kibuuka
Uganda Peoples' Defence Forces

INTRODUCTION

"Africa is unhistorical with an undeveloped spirit still involved in the conditions of mere nature; devoid of morality, religions and political constitution. Therefore, the African has not reached the level of realizing his own being; he has not yet realized his person... The African is a natural man in his completely wild and untamed state."

These quotes from the writings of Friedrich Hegel define a receptive trap into which many so-called African intellectuals fall as they frantically struggle to prove and validate by any means possible the ancient and pre-colonial brilliance of a continent. For one would imagine that these echoes of vibrant but past civilisations would awaken their pride and make them optimistic that a progressive future is possible. But sadly these intellectuals do not even suspect how the subtle distraction concealed in these quotes diverts them from the object of their real mission.

Luckily a new generation of African intellectuals seems to have understood this. Its members gaze in amusement at this highly dogmatic portrait painted from a racial perspective. They further refuse to address this old-fashioned topic, since it is not even capable of mitigating the unspeakable pains of 'this Africa of worse calamities'. "Africa did it, Africa can do it again!" should be their motto when African historians such as Joseph Ki-Zerbo and Cheich Anta Diop have long completed the scientific task of proving the ancient predominance of Africa.

The real topics should revolve around questions such as: How do we industrialise Africa? How do we fight against its endemic corruption? How can we prevent and settle armed conflicts on the continent? Why do so many Africans become disorientated, even maladjusted, once back from the western universities? Why are we so powerless in front of our diluted normative social guidelines? How do we contain religious fundamentalism and fanaticism? Do we really fight xenophobia and tribalism?

How deeply do we comprehend the principles of the social contract? How do we hold back and eradicate the pandemics of various diseases? How can we abolish poverty? How do we contain bad citizenship and insecurity?

Here we are immersed in the views of implacable Afro-pessimists and other fatalists whose only argument in explaining the backwardness of Africa is the cumbersome presence of a certain haunting 'western vampire'. "Africa is eternally condemned to serve, feed and be exploited by western imperialism" they claim. And, in truth, from careful observation of the social and political policies and practices of African regimes, we must conclude that we, Africans, need self-flagellation in order to awake up and clearly see our own responsibilities in the failure of our so-called 'westernized African countries'.

The sole aim of this book is to point out some of the daily behaviour patterns that Africans should rid themselves of in the process of ensuring that the slogan 'building a better life for all' becomes a reality.

Jean-François Kouadio
Tananarivo, Madagascar

CONTENTS

An Endemic Crisis

[...] Incivility and illiteracy are the African politician's choicest raw materials [...]

Ivorians have come to realize that their country is not the poorest in Africa. The most underprivileged social class that fidgets at the slightest sign of upheaval shown by an opportunistic opposition soon puts aside its qualms. Still, as a corollary to poverty, insecurity is rampant. Gangsters openly challenge the public authorities by hijacking grocery stores – even next to police stations.

In truth, the pauperization of Ivorian society is best illustrated by the flagrant lack of civility. At 10pm a man who stands alone at a bus stop will rarely hesitate to unfold his dick and pee on the empty seats. Why? Because there is no toilet anywhere near the bus stop and he will not run the risk of missing his bus by walking off and looking for a proper toilet. If anyone challenges him, all he will say is: "Well, it's not my fault if the State refuses to build toilets at the bus stop; plus by tomorrow morning, the seats will have already dried." If such a person also feels like 'emptying his stomach', he will not hesitate to do so on those same seats. Of course, the following morning, assaulted by the breathtaking stench of the human waste shamefully dropped at such sensitive spots, passengers will stand dozens of meters away. Moreover, it is barely understandable that in this age of the Internet, some still scratch out the seal mark left on the post office's stamps to re-use them. What a laugh!

In the business center of Abidjan, the capital city, the streets are cluttered with beggars. You'll find groups of blind people (or so they appear to be), lepers and the one-armed sitting at the corners of every intersection and begging in a strange and aggressive manner that is close to hijacking. Some clever people simulate an infirmity and mingle with those who have chosen to sell their honor and dignity for a few pitiful coins. Now years ago, in the wake of unceasing complaints by tourists, the public authorities decided to react. Police were deployed to frighten and disperse the beggars with the result that passersby saw the most unbelievable spectacle. With the boldness of perfectly trained Olympic champions, the 'physically disabled', including the supposed blind, stopped their comedy and set off in a high-speed sprint with the police officers on their heels. Instead of using their robust hands for productive enterprises in the deserted farms of the rural areas, they simply buried them under their shirts to simulate an infirmity.

Indeed, in Ivory Coast, severe economic crises inspire the population with malicious but ingenious ideas. Some will pour egg yolk into their eyes and make them appear milky as if stricken by severe conjunctivitis or an inflammatory cataract. After this they'll be escorted by a young nephew and sit expectantly on the sidewalk of any busy street and, thanks to their superb camouflage, be assured that no passerby will hesitate to throw a coin into the collection bucket. Then, returning home after a few hours, they simply rinse off the milky yolk and restore their vision. The following day another drop in each eye will prepare them for 'work'.

After the muscular explosion of police activity, the beggars would leave their 'work stations' for two or three days. Certainly by the fourth, they are back on the streets. In fact, they follow a simple logic: if religious law prescribes alms as a key pillar of belief then there should surely be someone to collect them and in so doing maintain a God-fearing population. But the most notorious lack of civic consciousness is shown by schoolboys and students. They will stand on the roof of a fast running school bus and perform acrobatics as proof of their toughness. However, the bus seats were not made for tough guys of their calibre. A quietly seated boy will be mocked by his peers for being too formal; he who is not a bully is automatically seen as a coward. The number of reported deaths due to this mentality is simply deplorable. For such youth, bogged down in the infancy of human development, good school results are no longer seen as an ideal goal. Such values having been jerked upside down, he who sees things the wrong way becomes a model for those who developed latent idiotic instincts that, up to then, social censure had managed to contain. Once such individuals hear that their country adheres to freedom of speech and to the charter of children or youth rights, they see in such opportunity the favorable moment to express their 'illness' and soon contaminate their classmates and the entire school. Thus a fatal 'informality' becomes entrenched.

In urban zones, the incivility is more pronounced. The lack of trust between poor parents and their increasingly demanding children sometimes forces the kids to seek their ideal outside their own homes. But this ideal, in a society of honest people, is not easily reachable. A kid has to have good school results if he intends to take serious revenge on the miserable life of his parents; a kid has to be taught not to cheat; he has to learn how to copy the example set by real idealists: right-thinking and honest people. He has to be taught why one should respect the public authorities.

Given the impossibility of meeting such basic ideals (which are not even faintly visible at the home of a father incapacitated by the worst urban misery), frustrated kids tend to rebel against the public authorities. If, in the worst scenario, in the absence of good school results, they are to drop out at the primary level, they become the most redoubtable opponents of all schooling. Anything relating to formal schooling embitters them and the public authority soon becomes the cause of their failure. As a result they refuse to comply with any public instruction even though some of them are clearly capable of seeing and identifying an ideal in life. Moreover, the disorder has the advantage of providing them with a circumstantial well-being such as the satisfaction of a number of primary physiological needs. For most of them, eating, drinking, sleeping and the pursuit of sex are the key, if not only, activities of life. Yet it is known, that if one has not been able to add value to one's immediate surroundings, one cannot not claim to have exceeded the basic limits of animal behaviour. Some of these young people are so hopeless and disappointed in life that they see death as redemption. Fatalism, the worst poison of the human psyche, turns their consciousness into a state of permanent stagnation.

Some intellectuals, fully conscious of the long-term danger of such a situation, commit the incongruity of presenting a lucid analysis in order to resolve it. They point out that the content of school curricula does not match the projects of development nor do they entice the curiosity or the effective participation of adolescent school kids. Only flagellation is used to 'assist' the slow or stubborn learner and so these kids end up suffering an inferiority complex and, in return, become aggressive. The intellectuals' analysis is unbearably accurate. And yet the pitiful inertia of the anti-progress mentality jeers at them. The situation, they point out, would worsen if one matured from childhood to adulthood without having fixed this crisis of adaptation. In this regard, examples of civil servants who spend their entire lives searching for corrupt petticoats to satisfy their gonads are countless. They tie themselves to thousands of concubines, investing their money in brothels and bars. Now, once retirement (towards which they make no preparation) looms, the State, the government, foreigners, the West become their toughest enemies. "France has robbed us," they cry. "The government is corrupt, foreigners are messing up the economy, they should be kicked out …" they bark unceasingly. And as a result they do not have enough time to maintain their numerous unplanned-for kids nor think of creating a subsidiary source of revenue to cover their retirement days.

To these groups should be added the females of Ivory Coast who are rightfully unwilling to fit into the social system designed for and by males. Sexism completely poisons the national education system. The content of the basic prescribed books is full of poisonous sexism which has for years been ignored or at best underestimated. 'Mom is cleaning the grounder', 'Here is daddy's beautiful motorbike', 'Daddy is sleeping in his hammock', 'Dad is watching T.V.', 'Julia is washing the pot', 'Sally is watering the garden'. These sentences are taken from the foundation level education program's reading book. As you will note, females perform all the exhausting household tasks; those presenting relaxation, rest, and beauty are the preserve of males.

The negative consequences of these apparently bland texts are very ruinous. Little girls, who meet for the first time in a formal school program, are convinced that they will never perform better than boys. Their still developing consciousness is overwhelmed by the idea (as manifested in their official reading books) that they will be confined to an inferior rank at the end of the long training process called school. And so they are bound to clean the compound, sweep the floor, maintain the garden, and cook the meal while little boys, future daddies, will be relaxing in their hammock, waiting for the meal to be served.

In the face of the catastrophic results the schoolgirls score, some disappointed parents decide to either not send their daughters to school or to withdraw them from the system after the first bad result. "You'll surely find a man to marry you," they assure the poor girl. "He'll take care of you and your kids." Such assurances summarize the plan most parents have for their daughters. As earlier stated, marriage for the Ivorian woman is a profession. Confined to a degrading form of dependence, most housewives are not free in a country where daily freedom is earned through material means. And this explains why all women's movements of emancipation fail to meet their targets. The famous Ivorian Association for Women's Rights only contributes to dislocating more families than it creates or maintains. At the end of an international colloquium on women's rights held in Abidjan, some tried zealously to put into practice the theories that European women extol. It was hardly surprising that the luckiest ones were simply beaten by their husband-employers and the rest were promptly dismissed from their household profession.

The incontrovertible point that this stunning backlash makes clear is that unless an enduring springboard for the emancipation of woman is properly set, it will be useless organizing symposia, seminars and colloquiums on these rights in Ivory Coast. Given the current role-distribution in Ivorian households, the possession of material means guarantees male superiority and prerogative. Weakened by men's material power, women are incapable of resisting capitulation. That is why it is not surprising to hear that the cost of renting the sexual services of an average woman in the bars of Abidjan fluctuates between two bottles of beer and a grilled fowl. In total, if sexism at school is not a calamity, as most education experts in Ivory Coast maintain, how come, with female birth rates exceeding males, female illiteracy is so disproportionately high? And so it is that the capacity for creation, the brilliant mind, the intuition and the dynamism of women that should be stimulated and converted into tools of development, is left dormant and unexploited and one is hence not surprised that it is quite common to hear housewives say, "Well, if the municipality refuses to collect the dustbin, I'll use the sidewalk drain – that will teach them a lesson." How to explain to such a woman that rubbish in the sidewalk drains attracts mosquitoes and malaria? Strangely, once infected by the anopheles' bites, they would turn around, shouting, "We're poor, sick and the government doesn't care about us!"

Overall, as in most African countries, Ivorian society is not trustworthy. One often sees a father in the company of his entire family getting onto a public bus without a ticket. And once the traffic police stop the bus for a ticket check, such father will abandon his kids and wife in the bus and jump through the window despite the fact that the ticket is something he can afford – for the bus ticket costs ten times less than his daily wine bottle. How is one to convince such a maladjusted citizen that the construction of public schools, roads and hospitals is partly financed by the value of the public bus ticket?

In Ivory Coast, sixty percent of the population is illiterate. The result is a vast number of maladjusted men and women who are incapable of taking care of themselves and thus eternally stagnate, and consequently, there being no other choice, become fully dependent on the public authorities. Indeed, at the age of forty, the most intellectually developed have the mental age of an adolescent and even at the age of seventy some are still not fully adult.

In truth, incivility and illiteracy are the African politician's choicest materials for manipulation.

The Voter of 'Washington'

Vote for the man who promises least
— he'll be the least disappointing.
Bernard Baruch

The sea
The green sea!
The green sea with its foaming waves
The green sea with its heaps of ropey weeds
And haunting monotonous voice
Sings and dances so lavishly
She dances and sings
To the enchanting rhythm of the tremulous wind
Rocking an array of frolicking golden coconut trees
Into frenzied fits
Under the peaceful glance of some quiescent peddler . . .

This splendid scenery displayed by the fringe embroidery of 'Washington', Abidjan's largest shanty town, is in truth a sham, a farce. Seen from far away, the shacks are like stacks of match boxes or cans left to the mercy of the angry sea waves. As you step into the neighborhood of 'Washington' at sunset, fear the looming crooked nights that haunt the interminable corridors of this "metal-sheet city". Resist the inaudible footsteps of the malignant spirit which parades throughout the night, proposing its pollutant sex for rental, offering its cheap alcohol that etches large wrinkles on faces within days.

One will often hear from afar a dying echo, the faint shout of a young woman, an accomplice to her own rape. Those who live in the servile sexual bondage and cravings for forbidden passions with minors, visit 'Washington' to try and quench at no cost the thirst of their insatiable testes. In the poverty-stricken brothels the customers of 'girls for collective use' embrace the stench, the filth, the joy. They make contact with fetid, smelly body fluids and wrap themselves with dirt-caked and coarse blankets that look as if they were used by coal miners.

Sometimes one will hear the bang of an over-zealous policeman's gun as it puts paid to a night owl. The stench of the drains, chock-full of human waste, assails the nose. The enclosures where insatiable maggots crawl over their daily bread alongside large, wet, bustling, insomniac black-and-blue-green houseflies are irresistibly drawn by the intoxicating fumes of this putrid waste.

In the middle of every compound stands a large metallic enclosure that serves as a toilet. In some of the walls some naughty children had drilled holes, through which they peeped to watch naked females shower in preparation for their clients. To the women, this is of no consequence. The animals – dogs, sheep and goats – snuggle close to their owners. Everyone steals in order to survive. Sex work had long deprived all twelve-year-old girls of their virginity. In the shanty of 'Washington' girls peddle themselves to passersby in exchange for a kilo of rice or meat.

There, misery has stultified people. A baby relieves himself; like a sparking firecracker loudly empties his stinky paunch, incubator of intractable amoebas. That's the price to pay when one gorges oneself with food destined for the trash bin. A loving mother, dining heartily at the scene, takes a loving look at this futureless kid. Truly, these shanty towns sprawling a long way beyond Abidjan, resemble a gigantic pyramid at the base of which numberless shacks are scattered. And so, in 'Washington', humankind has reverted to the stage of *Homo-habilis*. Poor families come to believe that, although having a shelter cannot be the alpha and omega of their lives, it is nonetheless the cornerstone and essence of their pitiful existence. "*I have built a shelter, therefore I am.*" In these shantytowns, 'shelter' is the word that gives them hope. The first priority thus is shelter, with food coming a close second.

'Washington' is also where Jules Kwao lives with his family. The fifty-two year-old artisanal fisherman, who is the head of the boatmen cooperative of the slum, has three sons. Tall and skinny with a pulled and hollow face, his minuscule mouse-like ears (which contrast with his bulky cheekbones) vaguely recall the features of an ancient Songhai warrior. Since he is lanky and unbalanced, as he walks his interminable legs seem to fall off his skinny body. His large and fan-like palms owing to the daily long hours of paddle strokes are rough, veinous and dark. Kwao is also the illiterate delegate of the ruling party in 'Washington' where his main role consists in *gathering* the "uneducated electoral cattle" during the MP's once-in-five years' visit to the slum.

Well aware that the gigantic and rotten shanty town is not an appropriate neighborhood to live and raise his offspring, Kwao has a secret plan to change his family's life. After all 'Washington' is nothing more than a pile of rusted metal sheets with no toilets or running water, quite beside being home to an extraordinary number of abandoned and very mangy dogs. One can certainly not live forever in this hell where the toughest criminals of Abidjan run to escape from police raids. Instead, he has always dreamt of living in Cocody, ten kilometers away.

Cocody is the upper class suburb of Abidjan where ambassadors, ministers and MPs comfortably reside. That includes Claude Samba, the MP of Port-Bouët commune – which includes 'Washington'. None of this was foreign to Kwao who clearly decided to seize the opportunity that could finally lead him to Cocody. His calculation was as simple as it was realistic: he will remind the Honorable MP, Claude Samba, of the critical political role he played in gathering his followers. He won't forget to remind the politician of the scholarship the latter promised his son a year ago during a high school science award ceremony. Kwao's elder son had, indeed, the best science marks of the entire commune. Surely once the boy is back from Paris with his numerous university degrees, he would work in a renowned institution and live in Cocody as people of that caliber do. Then he, Kwao, would finally be delivered from the hell that was 'Washington'.

But today Kwao has to fulfill his part of the deal by voting and calling all of 'Washington' to vote for the honorable Claude Samba as the entire Nation renews its parliament. In return, the MP had promised five kilograms of rice and as much meat, in addition to a butane gas cooker, an electric lighter and some trendy T-shirts and caps for anyone who votes for his party, the Democratic Union. As the party representative in Washington', Kwao will supervise the distribution of the food. And given this task, he says to himself, "Ha! Meat and rice on the menu for a whole week! Meat and rice cooked on a gas stove! That should taste better! What a treat! No more darkening charcoal. Not to mention my son's scholarship!"

Today is thus exceptional. Dressed up in a colorful butterfly printed shirt, Kwao has breakfast with his wife and kids. He shares the compound with six other families. Next to the communal well, two meters away from them, a neighbor's skinny dog whose large red sores are invaded by a colony of ferocious flies, stares at the eating family. Its deeply dug sockets and visible ribs reveal its appalling diet. Not far from the scene, a vagabond cat meows ceaselessly. Its nostrils can no longer handle the smell of the garlic-marinated, grilled shrimp and sardines casserole/combo stew shared by the family. The transparent sauce is accompanied by a large and sticky piece of vitamin-free pounded cassava – the basic daily meal. The contrasting queasy stench of the ill-treated and faeces cluttered latrines nearby does not seem to bother the appetite of the eaters. Kwao has barely started his meal when Suleiman, one of his six neighbors, enters the compound.

"Salaam alekum," he says, jumping off his smoking and noisy motorbike. Kwao tried to reply to the greeting. A large piece of spiced cassava nearly suffocates him. His red eyes ooze from their orbits as if he is being choked. Fortunately a sip of water, drawn from the mug he quickly grabs, flushes the piece of cassava.

"Alekum Salaam," he finally replies, between two noisy belches.

"Kwao, the MP is at the polling station. He just voted. You better go now."

"This can't be," says Kwao, surprised. He then stands up, not without licking each finger of the right hand.

After two painful hours of waiting in queue because of the atavistic disorder that has forever characterized most African elections, he manages to access the voting booth. Once alone, he quickly flips through his brain to recall the voting *lessons* a city hall worker had taught him a week earlier.

"The only winning ballot paper is that of the Democratic Union, your party, which is symbolized by the elephant. Any other ballot paper with printed symbols like the tiger, the cat, the black key, the rising sun, the torch, and the palm trees belong to the country's enemies. They belong to the traitors of the republic. These are symbols of ingratitude, anarchy and war."

Without this lesson Kwao would certainly not have understood the complexity of the tropical vote. So once he has cast his vote, he stares with pride at his blue ink marked finger and exits the polling station. Stepping back into the vast compound, his eyes wander through the massive crowd of voters in search of the MP. But he sees neither a sign of a black Mercedes nor the horde of 'scavengers' and 'vultures' who usually escort the politician. However, a hundred meters from the primary school used as a polling station, he sees a five-ton truck invaded by a roaring and hysterical mob. As Kwao gets closer, he recognizes the flag of the Democratic Union hanging on the assailed truck. In the vicinity, several huge speakers bombard and spit out an infernal and cacophonic noise (said to be the latest single of the country's new star, the famous DJ, John Rafale).

Those embittered by the sudden and incredible success of John Rafale claim the artist owes it to a macabre ritual performed in Benin, the African voodoo headquarters. Some say he practiced necrophilia to get this high. Others say he had an incestuous affair with his own mother to mystically unleash his potential. Which is true? The surest and most credible story is that his current fame has gone beyond the country's borders.

As for Kwao, he soon realizes that the truck he sees contains nothing else than the victuals promised by the MP. But what a mess! A bunch of unchained 'gorillas', as those brainless bouncers of Abidjan are called, are trying to contain the hungry mob. But their batons and metal belts do not seem to intimidate the thronging mass.

Frustrated, Kwao shouts at one of the 'gorillas'.

"You there, I'm Kwao! I'm the area delegate. Let me pass."

"Say what?" screams back the bouncer.

"I say my name is Jules Kwao . . . the delegate . . ."

"So?"

"So give me my rice and meat! I voted!"

"Get back asshole!" the 'gorilla' shouts while pushing the crowd.

Kwao does not seem daunted as he tries to move forward. He sweats profusely as if a bucket of water was thrown over him. He still cannot understand why he has to fight for what is rightfully his. But he won't give up. Playing with his elbows, he strains to reach the truck which is already being ransacked by a bunch of ill-bred, starving kids. In spite of the compactness of the crowd, he would be foolish to turn back without his bag of rice. He would surely appear stupid to go home without his piece of meat and a gas stove. What would have been the purpose of voting? Go back empty-handed? "No, it's today or never!" he murmurs.

The chaos that perfectly rhymes with the unbearable blast of *John*

Rafale's cacophonic tune does not allow any communication or concentration in the throng. Despite his height, Kwao seems asphyxiated, surely because of the torrid heat generated by the agitated mob. Suddenly a projectile, probably a stone thrown from God knows where, flies over the crowd and lands on Kwao's nose crushing his left cheekbone. A thick stream of blood erupts from his left cheek and showers those around him. He collapses and faints. The hungry mob then stamps over him as it rushes to the truck of victuals. In the confusion some people say: *"I voted – it is my rice"*. Or *"Where is my meat?"* Or *"My lighter doesn't work."* Or *"Fuck off!"*

The scene looks like a herd of ecstatic and starving baboons assaulting a tree of ripe fruits.

In the stifling heat of his sheet metal house, Jules Kwao is recovering from his injuries. He is still tortured by a dreadful headache as if more stones were striking his skull.

Laid flat on his dried grass mattress, he asks his wife: "Is that you Aja?"

"Yes Kwao"

"Please switch on the lamp, Aja".

"Kwao, it is almost two o'clock in the afternoon, it is still daytime"

"But what's happening to me?"

"Kwao, you probably lost your sight."

Aja bursts into tears.

"What?"

"Someone threw a brick at your face," she continues, still crying.

"And the bag of rice?"

"Nothing."

"And the meat?"

"Nothing, Kwao. You should rest now."

At the general hospital of Port Bouët where Kwao was admitted to intensive care, the doctors could not save his left eye. Two weeks after being discharged, he still keeps a wet and bulky transversal compress on the left side of his hollow face. After hearing his story, a nurse at the hospital advised him to seek further assistance from 'his friend', the MP. Thus one Monday morning, following the nurse's advice, Kwao asked two of his

friends from the fishermen cooperative to escort him to the National Assembly building located in the CBD. Once there, because of his extreme
state of dejection, an amicable and sensitive security guard allows the
fishermen to access the MP's office.

Mr Samba's assistant is a charming, tall, slim, young woman aged
twenty-three. Her chocolate-like complexion testifies to a daily and as-
siduous use of cocoa butter skin polish. As the fishermen hit the reception desk, she stands up while pinching her sensitive nose. She seems
unable to understand how these crab and smoked fish stinking rustics
facing her can be part of the company her boss, Claude Samba, keeps.
Shocked, she inspects them – their uncombed and bushy grey hair down
to their dusty villager feet. Irritated by what she sees, she goes into the
aggressive mode that typifies the arrogant secretaries of Abidjan.

"Hey you, where do you think you're going? Can I help?"

Kwao's most learned friend replies, "Hallo, madam. Mr Samba
here?"

The illiterate fisherman's tone does not inspire any sympathy in the
secretary. She attacks while holding her high hips and pulling her neck.

"First, who the hell are you fools? And secondly, do you have an
appointment?"

"My name is Abu, this is Kwao, and he votes and is sick for vote . . .
this is . . ."

Enraged by what she believes to be a useless introduction, she now
screams above their heads, "For the last time – do you have an appointment?"

"But Kwao is Mr Samba's bother," Abu replies.

When the secretary hears the word 'brother', she pulls herself together and pointing at Kwao, says, "Okay, so this is Kwao . . . the sick
brother?"

"Yes Kwao, delegate Washington-Democratic-Union," Abu says
schematically.

"Fine, sit down and wait there. I'll be back."

And she disappears.

Having abandoned the fishermen in the waiting room adjacent to the
reception, she returns to her chair and quickly rings Mr. Samba.

"What! . . . No, no! . . . Who are these beggars in my office? . . . Kwa

. . . what? . . . Who the fuck is Kwao?" From where? . . . Washington? . . . Is he an American?" the MP went on yelling before abruptly hanging up.

Returning to the fishermen, the assistant says, "Well Mr Abu, what's your phone number? Mr Samba will call you once he's back from Italy. Thank you and now get out!"

Abundant, indeed, is the conman's harvest where fools set their camp.

The Radio Program

He knows nothing and thinks he knows everything
– that clearly points to a political career.
George Bernard Shaw

On the *Listeners News* program presented by René Thomas, the professors' debates turned around the social and economic downturn of Ivory Coast. The guests seemed to agree that the flagrant transgression of the social contract was proof enough that social guidelines had been diluted globally. They further explained that poor management had fatally succeeded in creating the misleading utopia of a casino economy and that the drastic drop of the citizen's purchasing power and the extreme timidity of the international sources of finance are the actual causes of Ivory Coast's severe economic downturn.

The décor at this academic debate had thus been set. But soon, out of nowhere, an amiable bricklayer would drop his trowel and his triangle and pop into the phone booth next to his workstation. He would take the floor to the disadvantage of those who really had something to say on the basis that he has the right to do so because Ivory Coast is, after all, a democracy, with freedom of speech and all that. Moreover, he has enough money to pay for a one minute phone chat and can therefore call the public radio station and join the professors in this very serious program.

"Hello? Is that the radio station?"

"Yes, sir," René Thomas will respond with great friendliness.

"Hello, can you hear me?!"

"You are live on air, sir. What political or economic formulas can you suggest to rescue the moribund national economy – even as we take into account the current rigid diktat of the Bretton Woods institutions?"

"I want to participate in the *Listeners News*," the bricklayer blabbers.

"You already are, sir . . . please continue."

"Yes, yes."

"What are your economic formulas?"

"I want you to play the latest single of Kofi Olomidé[1] or please feel free to play one song from Pépé Kalé's[2] previous album for me. I like it very much . . . I want to dedicate it to my girlfriend Alice Kouamé. She is currently sleeping at my place . . . then also do play another one for my friend Sékou who stays in …"

René Thomas will not let him say the name of the town where his friend Sékou lives.

"Dear sir, I believe that you're a little too early for our upcoming program. The music session presented by my colleague Miss Touré is on at eleven o'clock. But thanks for calling!"

"Allo? Are you going to play it, or what?" The bricklayer rambles on.

René Thomas reverts to his guests who are still busy discoursing on academic theories as the bricklayer in frustration hangs up after failing to have his favourite songs played on air. There are many who feel that, since they were not allowed to express themselves before the introduction of democracy, they should now be free to spit out what years of mono-partyism prevented them from saying – and thus there is no point in wondering whether they really have something to offer.

Another man, César Akon, more arrogant than a bloodthirsty mosquito, cousin of those so-called 'pre-democracy locked mouths', while claiming to be a radio presenter thanks to some sharp high-level nepotistic connections, howled ceaselessly every evening to the dismay of the general tax payers' ears. The radio host would generally not end this monotonous speech before another listener, tortured by his insipid performance, called in.

"Allo," the caller would say. "This is Kèlètiki, Dauda Kèlètiki. I'd like to take part in the game, sorry . . . I mean, to *participate* in the program."

"Well, thanks for correcting yourself. We are indeed *not* playing! Now, if I may ask my question straight away . . . what do you think Mr Teddy should do? His wife cheated on him. Should he kick her out the house?"

"Listen boy, I did not attend formal schooling. I am eighty-seven years old. I have thirteen children; the youngest is a high school teacher. The third one died during the Liberian civil war. Ah, the lazy boy! He

---

[1]   Singer from the Democratic Republic of Congo

[2]   Congolese musician

was not the hero I have been all my life. During the Algerian civil war . . . ooh la-la, my goodness, who can believe me today? If not for my great helpful hand, the Algerians would certainly have massacred the French army in 1975.[3] That is where I met Ramshad, a woman, a beautiful Algerian . . . ha-ha-ha Ramshad! She desperately wanted a child from me. And she was dead right to demand that because at that time all manner of women were crawling on their knees to my doorstep. Ah, the great Kèlètiki that I used to be! But Ramshad . . ."

Vexed by this irrelevant story, the radio host soon loses his cool and cuts him short.

"Sorry, Mr Kèlètiki, please revert to our topic of tonight."

"I'd like to. But I just need to complete this story, my boy."

"Sir," says the radio host; "let me perhaps rephrase: should Mr Teddy leave his wife because she cheated on him?"

The caller still ignores him and carries on, "As I was saying, during the Algerian war, after freeing the French army from a deadly Algerian offensive, I ..."

"Mr Kèlètiki, I'm afraid I'll have to end this chat," counters the radio host.

"And for what reason would you do that? I have a radio and T.V. license. I am a taxpayer. No one can ever deny me this right! We are in a democracy. I will say what I please on a damn public radio station because in this country . . ."

"Goodbye, Mr. Kèlètiki!"

"'Allo? 'Allo? The son of a bitch! He really has hung up on me . . . and just when I was about to bring him into the light. Ha, but that's not surprising! Thieves are always scared of the light. What do I care?" says Kèlètiki before banging down his old phone.

Dauda Kèlètiki clearly did not know or did not care about the principle of the program called *The Solution*. Listeners in need would arrange an appointment with the radio presenter, come to the station and share their daily worries. They would expect sleepless listeners to suggest practical solutions to their problems. It was often said that César Akon, the radio host, had managed to re-unite some divorced couples and as time went by the popularity of the program grew beyond all expectations. In particular, the studio phone would ring endlessly when the topic of the

---

[3]   The Algerian civil war referred to, was already over since 1962.

day was sex – a subject that delighted his listeners more than any other.

On Thursday, May 10, César Akon or Mr. *Solution* invited a number of homosexuals, who in spite of the era of democracy, the freedom of speech etc. still felt the sting of public condemnation and censorship. There were three of them in the studio that day. The host, naïve as a fifteen-year-old, believed that the profile of his guests would attract either his listeners' curiosity or at least their usual sympathy. In fact, the men, who were members of an informal group, were secretly hoping to create the country's first gay rights organization by launching it during their interview. They hoped to see gay marriage legalized in the near future.

"Good evening, ladies and gentlemen," the host began. "Faithful listeners of *The Solution*, thanks for choosing our program. Tonight we have three charming guests who I'll invite to introduce themselves to you right away. Let's perhaps start from my left . . . you are . . ."

"Aisha," responds the guest, his imitation of a modern, highly sophisticated lady sounding quite perfect.

"My name is Gertrude and I would like to marry a European," carries on the second one.

"And you, dear?" the host quickly addresses the third.

"My name is Rose. I would like to adopt a six-year old girl, thanks."

"Thanks, guys . . . in fact, should we say guys or ladies?"

"Ladies, please!" says Gertrude, who at first sight appeared to have an ascendancy over the other two.

"Great! Let us then stick to 'ladies'. Thanks for choosing our program for your struggle. I am sure our listeners will give us a ring shortly since this is such an important issue . . . 'Allo!"

"Is that *The Solution*?" an impatient caller asks.

"Yes. May I ask who is calling?"

"My name is Alphonse Douf, I am a high school teacher. Listen Mr. *Solution*, we all know that not everybody is intelligent enough to conceive of and host a good radio program. So please do us a favor and play some music instead of all this talking. We are truly sick to death of your bullshit gay stories! We are taxpayers and radio license holders. Beside . . ."

"Mr. Douf, I see your request as a sign of maturity. Thank you very much for calling."

The lines were buzzing – it was time to take another caller. "We have another person on hold. You are Mr. . . . .?"

"No, I am Mrs. Kassé," goes a very motherly voice.

"We are listening to you, Mrs Kassé."

"I would first like to know if your guests believe in God."

"I'm a Catholic and I go to church every Sunday," replies Gertrude.

"I have received my baptism," Rose adds.

"I am a Muslim," concludes Aisha.

The radio host then says, "Well, Mrs. Kassé, can we carry on?"

"Yes, this detail is important to me because I believed your guests need God in their lives."

"Why not? And I am sure God will help them launch their first gay pride event. Thanks for your call."

Almost immediately another call comes through.

"Yes, 'Allo!"

"Sir, I am pastor Dede. I think gays are sick."

"And may I please know what they are suffering from?"

"They are suffering from Satan," the pastor serenely continues.

"My sincere apologies, pastor. I honestly didn't know that Satan was a disease," the radio host said.

"Wait, hear me out. I mean they are *possessed* by Satan. The Bible says in Corinthians chapter . . . "

"Listen pastor, what do you propose? What is your solution?"

"Well, I offer to exorcise them, to provide a deliverance session."

"Good, and after the session, the gays of this country will be allowed to get married. Thank you pastor, we got your point. 15 20 15 is our phone number. You can call us if you have a solution for our guests tonight...Allo?"

"Yes, 'Allo!"

"Please introduce yourself and give us your solution."

"I do not need to introduce myself. You surely know me by now," says a vaguely familiar voice.

"Go ahead then."

"Bright! Firstly, you owe me an apology, my boy. The last time I called, you cut the line before I could complete my story. Secondly, understand we are in democracy; listeners have the right to talk, especially when they are as old as I am."

"Sure, where were we?" the radio host asked.

The listener, happy to have been so cordially treated, clears his throat as a sign of victory and soon comes back to his previous love story.

"So, as I was saying before you interrupted me, during the Algerian war, after I had heroically survived three decisive battles, I came back home with Ramshad. If you drive to Abobo, the suburb where I am ... by the way, very popular ... you will see at the end of *Williams Peet* Street, an old Chevrolet. I bought this car in Algeria after the war. I bet it can still run if I fill the tank and change the engine. It's a pity I can't afford to buy some fuel nowadays. I can hardly believe that a litre of unleaded fuel used to cost only 3 Francs C.F.A before the war ... Well to cut the long story short, this car still runs. But, in fact, Ramshad ..."

"Please, Mr. Kèlètiki! I beg you to stay focused on our topic of tonight!"

"Hey, my boy! Do not interrupt me again. I am eighty-seven and have thirteen kids. I was a French, Indochinese and Algerian war veteran. I have five war medals and countless decoration ..."

The radio host, amused by this irrelevant tale that he knew in fine detail, decided to keep quiet. He was sure that his faithful listener, Mr. Kèlètiki, would run out of breath with so much bawling. But the more Kèlètiki spoke, the more he was inspired.

"So once back from Algeria, where my first son still works, I decided to create the association of war veterans. We decided to focus on ..."

Beep ... Beep ... Beep ... goes the hung-up handset.

"'Allo? 'Allo? The mother fucker! These youngsters know nothing but they refuse to learn. Trust me – I will get this garbage to listen to me one of these days."

That was how wise man, Kèlètiki, hero of the Second World War, veteran of the Indochinese war and the Algerian war of 1975, was complaining. He really was famous in Abobo, where he lived. Who did not know the most unrepentant adversary of the political system? Who had never heard of the most experienced democrat, the oldest, the most cultivated of his generation, the 'left-wing' intellectual? The man who knew yesterday, today and tomorrow's generation.

During the day, in bed or at his dinner table, on his way to the mosque or at any grocery store, his war medals always proudly hung on his chest. Was a neighbor beating his wife? Kèlètiki the democrat and righter of wrongs would want to know why. Then he would pick up one of the guns (of a very old model) he was said to have brought from Algeria, and burst into the neighbor's house to frighten and disperse the belligerents. If birds were disturbing his siesta, Kèlètiki would open fire at his mango tree, dispersing thousands of feathers. Of course, no neighbor would dare complain about his shot. So he was right in trying to assure the radio host that he was well known – at least where he lived.

On the same radio station there was also a slot for literature, featuring poetry, short stories and so on. Mariel Adu, a full-time high school teacher, hosted these sessions in the evening. For most listeners her program was one of the most boring sessions on the station. To understand the influence of Parnassus on Baudelaire's[4] poetry and its qualitative innovation in modern literature is not a subject of great interest for most listeners who were rather drawn to engaging stories offered by programs such as *The Solution, The Night Kiss, The Music Session and The Secret of Night* where there was no need to think and during which one could yawn and belch on the phone in the name of democracy.

Fortunately Mariel Adu came to realize this. Instead of offering the microphone to just a handful of scholars, she decided to allow interested listeners to call and read their poems or short stories live on air. In the landmass of Ivory Coast no greater literary productivity had ever been showcased; never before had greater democrat-poets so usefully occupied the national airwaves. And nothing testified to this better than the following fruitful exchanges between Mariel Adu, the presenter, and Mr. Koné, a listener.

"Good evening, Madam."

"Good evening, sir."

"I'd like to *tell* my poem."

"Please recite it rather."

"Well, here we go. The title is *Fatu, my dear darling.*"

"Oh, yes?" The presenter doubtfully asked.

"Sure." the democrat-poet confirmed, and proceeded to recite:

Since Saturday, 8 September
When you left our house for
The funeral of your mother-in-law
I am still alone in our suburb
In our bedroom
Alone in my dreams
Alone with the children

---

[4] Charles Pierre Baudelaire, French poet (1821-1867), spearhead of Symbolism.

Ha! My darling
If you don't come back soon
I think I might be sick
Ha! Fatu, when you are not around
The sun does not shine properly
When you are not around
The moonlight is not clear

Beautiful night
Beatiful sun
Beautiful Fatu
Beautiful Futu[5]
Beautiful lady
Beautiful woman

Oh! Fatu my darling
Ah ! Fatu surplice
"Sorry ..." my accomplice
I am waiting for you
I love you today
Less than yesterday
More than tomorrow
"No, I'm sorry ..."
I love you today
More than yesterday
Less than tomorrow

Oh, Fatu
Ah, Fatu

"Mr. Koné?" The radio presenter asked, to make sure the highly lyrical poem had reached its end.

"Yes."

"Mr. Koné, was this supposed to be a poem or a letter?"

"A poem."

"Good night, Mr Kone!"

"'Allo? Allo? Shit! I wanted to explain my poem so badly. I will call

---

[5] Local pounded yam dish

back."

"'Allo? We have another caller on the line?"

"Yes, my name is Martin Poku."

"We are listening to you, sir."

"Good evening."

"And good evening to you, sir. Let's save time and listen to your text."

"Good Evening," says the caller.

"Sir, you've already said that. Would you please recite your poem."

"I am trying to. The title of my poem is *Good Evening*!"

"Oh sorry, let's then listen to *Good Evening*."

Good evening
Good morning
It is a late morning
Birds are singing in the sky
Fishes are dancing in the river
The rat is crying in its hole

Good evening
Good morning
What a late morning!

The presenter got fed up. She repeated the refrain of the poem.

"Birds sing in the sky and fishes dance in the river" . . . is that right?"

"Yes, and also the rat cries in its hole," completed the poet.

"And the rain falls from the sky and men walk on their feet" … what more Mr. Poku?"

"'Allo? 'Allo? I am not done!" the caller shouted desperately as the presenter disconnected the line.

"Yes 'allo, a new caller?"

"'Allo, my name is Mr. Kèlètiki," responded an already known voice.

"Ah! Mr. Kèlètiki, how's this evening treating you?"

"Fine, thanks."

"And what poem does Mr. Kèlètiki propose tonight?"

"Well, I'd like to elaborate on the modern origin of poetry."

"Ah, you mean the origin of modern poetry?"

"No!" Roars Mr. Kèlètiki. "I know what I'm talking about. I said the *modern* origin of poetry and NOT the *origin* of modern poetry. Because anything that exists has an origin. And anything modern has an ancient origin. Beside, any ancient thing is clearly wise. Originality comes from ancient times and ancient times are becoming original. You see, the difference is clear!"

"Um, well not really clear. But is that important anyway? Let's perhaps get back to ..."

"What?! I can't believe this!" Mr. Kèlètiki grumbled, stung by the presenter's comment. "You said what I am saying is not important?"

"No, it is a misunderstanding. I mean ..."

"What's the meaning of this? I wonder how you fuckers get recruited at this fucken public radio station."

"No, sir, I mean ..."

"Shout your big mouth and listen to me! I am old enough – I deserve to be treated with respect."

"Mr. Kèlètiki, please ..."

"Listen! I am a Second World War, Algerian war and ..."

"Once again I am sorry Mr Kèlètiki, let's perhaps come back to poetry."

"What for? Do you think poetry is better than being a war veteran?"

"Best regards to your family Mr. Kèlètiki" murmurs the radio host before hanging up without alerting the embittered listener.

"'Allo? 'Allo? No one can stop freedom of speech this way. Put me back on!"

And so, yet again, Mr. Kèlètiki, savior of France, custodian of our tropical democracy, would rage on about the criminal nature of the national radio station. Crazy youth! Had it not be for the rudeness of the so-called 'radio presenter', Mr. Kèlètiki would have delivered a poetic dissertation of an excellence not even Charles Baudelaire would have matched.

Kabaforo

Part 1

[...] He came to the Ivory Coast to wash, clean, cleanse, bleach, purify, disinfect, sanitize and 'whiten' the niggers; well, to turn them into human beings [...]

Three hundred kilometers west of Abidjan is Kabaforo, the headquarters of the Jakuni clan. Here the traditional culture is at its purest and needs to be approached with caution. In Kabaforo the priority is not farm work. It is rather the practice of fetishism and witchcraft. Here, people have from time immemorial practiced sorcery to kill time and to punish those who work too hard. In Jakuniland, magic has always been used as a source of entertainment. Indeed, one can go and discover this community where, according to the former French governor, the colonial project was a complete failure, a thorough waste of time.

On one occasion Anatole Poiriot, Ivory Coast's colonial administrator-general, wrote to the French Minister of Colonies based in Paris: "[...] *Sir we are wasting our precious time with the Jakuni. These people are the dregs of the Black race . . . perfectly lazy, the worst of the darkest Negroes that ever walked this earth. To put it bluntly, they are the sign of God's punishment to mankind [...]*"

After more than fifty years, the Frenchman got fed up. The Jakunis' general renunciation of Western education (with very few sending their children to school, and with these small numbers managing to evidence the highest dropout rate in the territory), their refusal to farm despite occupying the most heavily forested region of Ivory Coast, their entrenchment in a culture viewed as worthless by France, compounded by their refusal to use piped water and other amenities, all left the French wondering what to do with them. Upset, the colonial governor decided to remove whatever modern infrastructure had been built in Kabaforo. "*These savages do not deserve such luxury; the lazy man's stomach does not deserve the fruit of hard-working hands. Heine was right.*"

The story of a young southern policeman tells it all. Fresh out of police training school, Rigobert Banda requested to be sent to Kabaforo.

The day he received his posting instructions, Banda was ecstatic. He said to himself: "The time to bring civilization to Kabaforo has come! If I succeed it will indeed be a historic victory. My name will go into the annals of Ivory Coast's police force. What power can black magic have against my gun and baton?" He couldn't believe that many police officers had gone to Kabaforo swearing to defend the national police force at the cost of their own lives, only for them to turn into cowards. That was how audacious the freshly recruited policeman was. However, it must be said that, despite his naiveté, his desire to escape his own rural poverty and assist the Jakuni was genuine.

When he reached Kabaforo, he was surprised to discover that the police chief, his new boss, was a young man of his own age. Moreover, the police chief was famous in the entire province for his friendliness to both his colleagues and the villagers of Kabaforo. At the first meeting he had with Rigobert, the chief issued a warning.

"My dear Banda, as I have already explained to many of your predecessors, we are not in Kabaforo to work. We are here to wait for our wages. Do not be too zealous at your task. Why? Because we are in Kabaforo. No ID checks. No roadblocks. Do not swear at a Jakuni. On the contrary, be their friend. That is if you plan to have a peaceful life here in Kabaforo. Do you understand, sergeant?"

Rigobert could not hide his astonishment. He could not believe that even the police chief was a coward.

"But why?" he asked.

"When I arrived here three years ago," the police chief responded, "My wife wanted to start a business. She imported second-hand clothes and cheap jewelry from Liberia. She was quickly making headway . . ." Rigobert was listening intently to his chief's story. "But when the Jakunis discovered that my wife was doing well with her new business, problems started."

The police chief stopped. His eyes sharpened.

"She woke up one morning to find her body covered in incredibly large boils. I must confess that I have never seen such boils in my life!"

"Sir, it could have simply been an allergy."

"Believe me, we all thought it was. But the medical tests invalidated the allergy story."

"Is she still alive?"

"Yes, thanks to a powerful Jakuni priest, a man called Zakatu. He told me she was cursed."

"How did he know that?"

"Well, he cured her through a ritual that was as magical as it was strange. I later heard that Zakatu is a priest of their clan's god. He is so powerful that his glance can mummify any barking dog, or any snake or mosquito that dares attack him."

"Is this priest still around?"

"Yes, of course. And you'll meet him."

Rigobert Banda was very pleased that Zakatu, the sorcerer, was still alive. He welcomed the opportunity to test his bravery, his baton and his gun, against the sorcery of these savages. "This is all hot air! I will make sure all their nonsense ends!"

Weeks later despite a spate of warnings by his chief, Rigobert took his gun and his torch and went out on patrol. His intention was to start on his noble mission and bring light and civilization to the savages! It was around eight o'clock in the evening. In the misty darkness of the Harmattan he saw three silhouettes.

"Hey, you there!" he challenged. The prowlers stopped walking. The police sergeant bathed their faces with the bright light of his torch. "Your identification papers!"

The walkers didn't understand much of the French language and rather than apply themselves to learn more, they seemed rather busy looking for a way to disappear into the surrounding darkness. But Rigobert Banda had his right hand on his gun. And seeing this, quickly changed their minds. "Where are your papers?" "Where are your IDs?" Suddenly from his left appeared two more people on a bicycle. "Hey, you two! Come here! Your papers? A real man carries an ID. Where the hell are yours?"

In reply there was only silence. The sergeant soon realized that he was wasting his time trying to talk to either deaf or illiterate savages.

"Strip off your shirts!" he ordered. "Blockheads!"

Then he noticed the innumerable amulets that girdled his captives' chests. The impressive amulets festooned the whole of the upper body, from the hips to the armpits with others running diagonally across the trunk – and also covered the arm from the elbow to the armpits. Furthermore, their wrists were weighed down by the amulets. Indeed, the five men who had fallen into the jurisdiction of the most conscientious sergeant in the national police force were genuine initiates. But Rigobert

Banda was offended. With the tip of his baton he lifted one of the amulets.

"Jesus Christ!" he exclaimed. "Just look at these stinking amulets! Let's go! Lead the way!"

In single file, herded and intimidated by Rigobert Banda's gun, the men headed to the police station. When they arrived, they were locked up without explanation. The stench, the darkness, the mustiness, the coldness of the cell, the angry wasps, the bloodthirsty mosquitoes, the voracious bedbugs, the transparent salamanders, the cockroaches crawling with their families – all welcomed the captives. The night was long and sleepless. They sneezed incessantly. By early morning, their bladders were close to exploding.

The following day Rigobert Banda summoned his boss to see his captives, as proof of his hard work. The police chief took one glance inside the cell and said, "Sergeant, free these men immediately! It's an order!"

The sergeant had since his arrival in Kabaforo never seen his young boss in such a foul mood.

"But sir, these …" he tried to complain.

"I am saying it for the last time, free them now!"

When Rigobert opened the entrance to the filthy cell, the police chief smiled broadly and said in an extremely friendly tone that surprised the sergeant, "Well, well, my dear Zakatu. How are you, my brother?"

Rigobert's heart missed a beat. Standing in front of him was none other than the infamous Zakatu, the very man it was alleged no dog could bark at or snakes dare bite.

The priest threw a look at the sergeant. The police chief tried to divert his attention from the priest by adding, "Look Zakatu, my brother, he is a newcomer. He knows nothing about police rules. Forgive this novice. My brother, how is your health?"

Zakatu didn't respond. The police chief continued, "Ha, my brother, Zakatu, I owe you a personal apology. I'll come to your house tonight to make up for this misunderstanding. In the meantime, please take this banknote to your wife on my behalf."

The priest was still silent, and so were his friends. Then he took a deep breath and simply said, "You are dead."

"Zakatu! Zakatu! Please wait, don't go yet, my brother," the police chief pleaded.

No doubt about it – he was trying really hard. But Zakatu and his friends did not seem to have much interest in what he was saying. They left the police station with sinister expressions on their faces.

"What is the matter with you, sergeant?" the police chief asked, furious. "What did I tell you?"

"But sir…" Rigobert Banda tried to explain even as he suddenly started to sweat.

"I swear Zakatu will kill you today if he sets his mind on it. Stay right here; I'll speak to him alone. We might still have time to undo his curse."

After two hours of negotiations and supplications with Zakatu, the police chief returned to his office. He found Rigobert Banda slumped over his desk, with mouth agape. He was breathing in fits and starts. His stomach had swollen and was the size of a carnival balloon; his eyes had bulged as if he was being strangled, and he could not talk. His colleagues stood around him, looking bewildered and helpless. But more was to come: he started shaking like an epileptic, saliva dribbled from his mouth and he vomited without stop. His powerless and terrified colleagues believed that Rigobert was fatally condemned for their experience told them that the Jakuni's curse had no mercy. How many of their friends and family members had died because they wanted to fight the Jakuni's traditional way of hunting – which was to set hectares of forest on fire even if only to corner and capture a single palm rat? Another reason for their deaths had been their opposition to the rampant smuggling which took place across the nearby Liberian border.

"Sergeant? Sergeant?"

The police chief's pleas were in vain. Rigobert was semi-conscious. He heard a cacophony of buzzing sounds. He was still vomiting. His stomach was swollen. The weight of this skinny police officer seemed to have doubled in less than an hour; and the more weight he gained, the more difficult he found it to breathe. Soon he was grunting like a pig, hot sweat streamed down his face until he completely lost consciousness.

The police chief said to the officers standing at Rigobert's 'side', "Let's all do something to save this idiot. Zakatu wants the sum of a hundred thousand francs. That's the price of a white sheep and a crate of whisky to make up for the damages he and his friends suffered. Let's all contribute something. I'll start with fifty thousand francs. And you, my adjutant?"

"I'll give twenty, sir."

"Who else? What about you, Lieutenant? Please help, he's your colleague, give something, please!" And when more contributions were made, he shouted out, "Great! That should do."

People said that once Zakatu the magician-priest received the money, he simply straightened out the neck of a magic toucan suspended from the roof of his hut. He had actually blown poisonous air into Rigobert's throat while calling the callous spirit of death to embrace the sergeant. People also said that, at the very moment the toucan's neck was being straightened out, the sergeant recovered. Rigoberto later visited the powerful Zakatu to thank him for having spared his life and handed him the whole of his miserable monthly salary. Afterwards, he requested and obtained his transfer far, far away from Kabaforo.

Of course, such occult practices in Jakuniland have hindered development in the entire region; the Ivorian government simply ignores these enemies of agriculture. All the green lands in the deep forest where they live have been declared a 'sacred forest' by the patriarch of the community. The lands are only used for ritual sacrifices. Their God doesn't like farm work. He even hates it. He doesn't seem to like schools either for the vast majority of the few children in primary school were not Jakunis but the children of civil servants temporarily based in Kabaforo.

Part 2

The French colonial governor, Anatole Poiriot, said in a report to the Minister of Colonies based in Paris: "[...] *These Jakunis are actually sub-humans, latecomers to the human race. The value of this clan doesn't exceed zero. Sir, how can we convince them that agriculture is good for their filthy and rotten Negro mouths? How can one refuse development? But then I think this clan is incapable of distinguishing Good from Evil. Let's simply say they are just 'pre-Adamic' monsters, nothing better* [...]"

But then despite these conclusions, Poiriot, based in Abidjan, dispatched a punitive expedition to Kabaforo to try and frighten the Jakunis into taking up agriculture. The notorious and extremely brutal provincial French commander, Claude Lecul, was entrusted with the mission of leading the expedition. Lecul, a former First World War veteran, had come to the Ivory Coast to 'wash, bleach, clean, purify, disinfect and whiten the niggers' – and so turn them into human beings. And wasn't it under his supervision that the railway line that runs from Abidjan to the north was built? And who abolished cannibalism in the south-east of Ivory Coast? Why, Claude Lecul!

About the Jakuni clan, Mr Lecul had said to Anatole Poiriot, "Believe me, sir, niggers should be branded with a red-hot iron, and I can assure you, it works."

Mr Poiriot had a great deal of trust in Lecul. He knew what the man was capable of. The governor advised Lecul to start by negotiating with the Jakuni clan. Lecul put together a unit of thirty French soldiers and set out. But despite the fact that they had no guns or grenades, the Jakuni refused to negotiate. Thereafter, having arrived in Kabaforo, fifteen of the French soldiers died, one after the other, from causes that have to date not been established. Lecul, upon returning to Abidjan, thoroughly upset by his first real defeat, asked a French doctor to examine the corpses of the dead soldiers in order to determine the cause of death.

The doctor was to the point. "They all received electric shocks," he said.

"What? How's that possible? These animals don't even have a single paraffin lamp. What electricity are you referring to?"

Although skeptical of the doctor's diagnosis, Lecul, feeling that enough was enough, requested and obtained from Paris the toughest division of the French army. The French met the Jakuni with utmost force; they burnt down their huts and sacred forest, left behind countless bodies and arrested one of the most notable patriarchs of Kabaforo. This patriarch was said to be the mastermind behind all the Jakuni witchcraft. The soldiers tied the great doctor like an antelope, and to prevent him from escaping by using his magical powers, put him in a sack. After throwing away his amulets, the sack containing this supreme mediator inbetween the Jakuni and their gods, was locked up in the basement of the colonial garrison building.

The following morning, the commander asked the guards to open the sack. The guards formed a large circle around the captive. But, as soon as they opened it. The commander jumped back.

All the magician wore was a loin cloth made out of tree bark. His head was dusty. His mouth was very wide. His narrow forehead was covered with deep wrinkles. His nose was flat as if it had been shattered by a heavy blow. His red eyes were hidden deep in their sockets surrounded by grey, bushy chimpanzee eyebrows. He had a squint in his left eye. His temples were furrowed by the unforgiving years of possessing and practicing fatal powers. A goiter, traversed by a swollen vein, bulged on his neck. As for his skin, the great witch doctor was so black one got the impression he had just been hauled out of the depths of a coal mine. From the floor of the basement where he was sitting, he looked up, astounded, to be in the middle of this unaccustomed circle then suddenly tried to say something in his mother tongue which, to his listeners, appeared to be utter gibberish. He then bared two long, wicked yellow teeth for all to see. It was quite obvious that no toothpick had ever touched those teeth.

Claude Lecul stared biliously at the witch doctor. "Well, well, well: Here is our great personage . . . the untouchable and undefeatable enemy of development . . . Ha! Ha! Ha! Isn't that beautiful?"

While Claude Lecul was laughing at him, the witch doctor tried to stand up. The guards brutally grabbed his shoulders and held them firmly. Claude Lecul continued, "I cannot believe this! This is incredible, absolutely incredible! How can such a baboon carry the honorable title of 'chief'? But then again – why should this be incredible? Logically this *is* the chief of the baboons. So, yes, guards, keep the baboon safe. I am sure the Governor would like to see it."

Later, the governor had the 'baboon' photographed and the picture sent to Paris, followed by another report:

> [...] Mr Minister, if this man's description was given to me by a French journalist, I would have undoubtedly suspected the pitiful racism that France, the mother of the universal liberty, has always denied. But I saw the medicine man with my own eyes. He has an exceptional physique. You may confirm it from this photograph attached to my report. It was taken shortly after he was captured. Thus, the medicine man, who is also chief of the Jakuni, the public nuisance, is now in good hands. Kabaforo's march towards development is now irreversible. [...].
>
> Please trust my indefatigable diligence and welcome the expression of my highest consideration.
>
> **Anatole Poiriot**
> *General Governor of the colony of Ivory Coast*

The Initiation

Part 1

A true initiation never ends.
Robert Anton Wilson

The heavy rains of Kabaforo lash down on hamlets, hills, valleys and plateau. The weakened soils struggle to absorb each and every raindrop while the long dried-up plants stand patiently, hoping to bear the fruits that will keep the Jakuni clan alive. Surely the rains come each season to wash away their misfortunes and offer abundance! And so the Jakuni cannot wait to see those first heavy drops mark the beginning of the New Year. Even those Jakunis scattered in faraway places such as Paris, London, Washington or Abidjan will return for this festival for they still believe that their absence from the homeland will irritate the gods. And among those who crawled along to rural Kabaforo this rainy season to receive the favors granted by the regional gods, was Roger Guéyo.

Guéyo was the military officer who had tried five years earlier to overthrow Dieudonné Baziana, the current president. As a former national army commander, he had been privileged to be the right-hand man of the country's first president. Those jealous of his success claimed that in the French army (where he had started his career), he had only been a cook; some said, just a driver; others that he had been a 'cannon cleaner'.

Roger Guéyo would later be promoted by the first president to the highest echelons of the army despite his frequent transgressions against Molière's language.[6] The colonel-major, head of army that he was, knew very little French. All his speeches in the barracks were occasions for laughter and entertainment. Only official duties can force a man to offer himself up as a laughing stock – as frequently occurred in Guéyo's case. So it was not strange that he would have liked to be silent. But as a chief, one has to talk, make speeches on television, on radio, in newspapers. All this was a nightmare for one who could not articulate two sentences without making mistakes and who, in retirement, became so taciturn

---

[6]   The French language

that he often revealed the comical character he was shaping out to be.

In the Jakuni language of his people, *Guéyo* means 'son of thunder'. As a retired military officer, he could spend quality time with his wife, Rosalie, during the period of the festival when both young women and men were initiated. Those who like to poke their noses into other people's affairs would say Roger was infirm. Some maligned Rosalie for, as they claimed, going around sleeping with the young businesspersons of Abidjan. Still others claimed that Roger's last son was not his at all.

Now Rosalie was present this rainy season to support her husband. In the Jakuni region, all believed in fetishes and they undertook nothing without one. It was common to find a schoolboy rolling up his shirt so his mate could admire the chain of amulets wrapped around his hip. Or a drunkard sauntering across the streets of Abidjan, who, after being nearly crushed by a speeding car, would sober up and immediately consult a priest so that he may stave off 'the spirit of accident' that would surely haunt him.

Roger Guéyo was no exception; he wasn't the type to turn away from his culture. So he came to this rainy season festival to warm up his own amulets. And as a man who savored challenges, he offered to try a special ritual called Ritual of the Son of Jakuni, upon completion of which, a special benediction would be granted to the worthiest son of the community. Each candidate had to show penitence and extreme humility during the course of the ritual. Though he happened to be the President of the Republic, he was required to bend down to earth if he was to enjoy the graces of the gods, and humble himself, eating with his bare hands and sharing the same table with his fellow contestants. As for Guéyo, it meant plunging his hand into the same bowl with his ten-year-old nephew. Here in Jakuniland, humility preceded glory.

Rosalie, too, with so many maidservants, prominent as she was in the upper-crust of Abidjan and Parisian society, had to play her part for the ceremony's success. With her bare hands she cooked a dish of smoked porcupine with which Guéyo stuffed himself at the beginning of the ritual, watering it down with plenteous palm-wine as was customary.

For his next challenge, Guéyo chose to climb the thorny and sacred tree. The gods agreed to entrust their power and this mission to Roger Guéyo, because the time had come to wash away the innumerable humiliations suffered by the Jakuni who live in virgin forest and were hungry because their regional god prohibited them from farming. This has been an ancient belief and one that no modern law can change.

Another interesting result of this prohibition was that the president of the republic, Dieudonné Baziana, and his nepotistic brothers, who live in air-conditioned mansions in the capital city, had been squandering the public funds that would have been allocated to the region thus making doubly sure that the Jakuni people would starve. But really, to be truthful, they were not alone in dishonoring the Jakunis. In general, in Ivory Coast, every odd or funny story related to a *savage* begins with "Once upon a time, a Jakuni . . ." or "a stupid man, pardon, a Jakuni . . ."

"We are fed up! Go and avenge us, Roger Guéyo! Your time has come!" assured the patriarch.

On the eve of his 'thorny tree climbing', the elders took him to the forest for initiation. There in the deep forest, a welcoming committee was waiting next to a wooden fire on which a juicy piece of meat was being grilled. Eight burly men, torches in hand, were dancing to the rhythm of a sacred drum decorated with a myriad of dusty yet symbolic mascots. Guéyo and four priests joined them. He sat bare-chested on the grass. While the dancing men circled him. Among them was the head-priest, who anointed Guéyo's body with a special oil said to be derived from human fat, they whitened his thorax and abdomen with kaolin powder and recited magical verses which he repeated after them. Suddenly, a man emerged from the bush. In his right hand he held a horn; in the other, a four-litre jerry can. The assembly turned to him. Raising the horn to his lips, he blew some heart-piercing, shrill sounds and the celebrants started to chant in an esoteric litany to the native god. Guéyo was uplifted; without doubt he was ready to fulfill his mission. The oldest priest among the nocturnal delegation made a sign to the man carrying the horn and the jerry can. Then a deep silence descended on the assembly – but not for long, as someone shouted, "Brothers! We are now going to refresh ourselves for the glory of our god!"

Kateka, the sacred beverage, went around the assembly. *Kateka* had always been a chief anesthetic among the Jakuni. Ages ago, when a warrior returned from a tribal war with an arrow lodged in his side, he was given some *kateka* so that the weapon could be removed with minimal pain. The drink was reputed to be so potent that one got drunk by simply sniffing it. No wonder it became the holy beverage of the gods. Guéyo, who was sitting in the middle of his initiators that festive night, was aware of the potency of the *katéka*. Granted, he had never tried it but he was accustomed to Scotch whisky and *Kateka*, as everybody knows, is the Jakuni version of Scottish whisky. Or is it that Scotch whisky, as some would have it, is the Scottish version of *Kateka*?

As the drink went round, roasted meat was served and what better delicacy than roasted placenta, the favorite meat of the gods? Guéyo picked a piece just as the others were doing and took a bite. He did not know the taste of the meat that had been set before him. But he ate it all the same, imitating the others who had already begun drinking. When the drink eventually made its way to him, he lifted it to his lips but no sooner had he sniffed it than the whole earth appeared to overturn beneath him. All around him, drinkers, already in various degrees of intoxication, were lying in a range of surprising postures. Guéyo cupped his head in his hands and reeled as if it was going to blow up. Without being aware of it, he was already in communion with his god, the energy of the spirit jolted him and he collapsed on to the grass.

That night Guéyo had a vision. The regional god was standing by his side, accompanied by some elders whom he vaguely recognized. One of the elders showed him the cup of the victors. Guéyo reached out, grabbed the cup and lifted it to his lips. He sipped the contents – wine of unequaled exquisiteness – which almost made him lift off the ground. He felt an overwhelming urge to empty the cup. But just before the wine made its way down his gullet, he heard a loud knocking, and the sensation subsided and he woke up in a strange hut in the village. The sun was already high in the sky. The bed pressed against his ribs as he sweated profusely. An inner voice reminded him that this was the price of the initiation. Still, his nakedness surprised him. A man entered the hut and Guéyo recognized him right away. He was one of his companions of the previous night. He held Guéyo by his shoulders the way one holds a child who has accomplished a great feat.

"Everything was perfect," the man said. "You climbed the holy tree to complete your initiation. Now, go back to the city and avenge us. Remember that you made this promise to the gods last night. Trust them, they will protect you. Remove the so-called president Dieudoné Baziana, that son of nothing! And bring us food; we are not allowed to farm this beautiful land. Now go, son, go and save your people!"

Part 2

After close to a century of colonization, France and her numerous governors had not fundamentally changed the Jakuni although, as years went by, the region boasted more infrastructure and public services than at the advent of occupation, which does not change the face that compared to the rest of the Ivory Coast, Jakuniland is the poorest and the most isolated. In Abidjan, any departmental head who wants to punish his subordinate will always say: "Next time you will be sent to Jakuni!"

Being posted there is truly considered a punishment. However, the government has built hospitals, primary schools, public water pumps and telephone booths. If this infrastructure did not exist, life in Roger Guéyo's land would seem to be a utopia. Its dense forest, seen from the sky, resembles a thick deep-green rug surrounded by a myriad of scattered mangroves. Its centennial trees could easily be mistaken for gigantic pillars watching over the eternal sleep of the gods therein. The long, robust lianas tightly twisted around the trees look like safety belts to ensure the peaceful rest of the sleeping myths and legends, far away from the profane's indiscreet watch.

This is also the time to celebrate the circumcision of young women. In Jakuniland, only after the ritual of circumcision is a young woman permitted to marry. The ancestral rules do not allow the circumcision of a non-virgin and that is the real significance of the ritual. Being a virgin underscores the morality of the families who brought up the young woman. Circumcision is painful, so only the brave endure it. A Jakuni mother brings honor to her clan when her daughter is found to be chaste. And she would rather die than stay alive without a child. Circumcision is thus the inevitable stepping stone to a Jakuni woman's honour.

The circumcisers gather the young girls at dawn. There are ten of them on this day, in a single room, covered with the ceremonial blanket. The circumcisers, septuagenarians whose fingers tremble like water in a bowl, murmur their reassurances:

"It is not painful."

"Your name and that of your family will be honored."

"After the rite, you won't be tempted to cheat on your husband."

"You will be different from the rotten women of the big cities."

"Those women don't have any kind of decency at all, they are not circumcised."

"They are nothing but bitches, constantly horny."

"They cannot hold back their excitement."

"Your husband will be proud of you."

"When your husband takes a second wife, you won't be jealous of her."

"Take heart, the spirit of the ancestors will honor you; will bestow his blessings upon the entire community."

"He will send more rain . . . and guess what, the rain will beget the marsh, and the marsh will host the fattest beautiful frogs, and the frogs are food, so there won't be any famine."

"You see, never again shall we starve, thanks to your commitment and courage."

In a corner of the room where these twelve or thirteen-year-old girls are assembled, they listen silently to the instructions. In spite of all the assurances offered, one can easily read the terror on each of these innocent faces. One of the 'experts' quietly insinuates herself into the poorly lighted room, a paraffin lamp in her hand. She murmurs something inaudible to a colleague. Everything seems ready. One of them, a well-known circumciser, holds in her hand an unsharpened kitchen knife with concave edges. Her family has jealously kept this tool for ages and she will bequeath it to her daughter before she goes to her grave.

Soon the 'experts' exit the hut followed by the girls; they are on their way to the sacred forest where the girls will, by the stroke of a knife, be turned into 'women'. The sun has not yet risen. It seems to be waiting for this rite to be performed before it can rise.

The very first girl to be circumcised – worthy daughter of the gods – does not feel the second bite of the corrosive, century-old blade. Strangled by excruciating pain, blood gushes out of her as her soul escapes her body.

"This one was given as a sacrifice to the gods. May his mighty name be magnified and may he protect us," remarks the circumciser.

The death of any young girl who expires before she can become a real Jakuni woman is believed to have been willed by the gods themselves; it is also believed that she will be happy to be welcomed into their everlasting realm. Nevertheless, what this particular death does for her fellow candidates is to weaken their faith. Yet the ceremony continues before the day breaks.

The day of the triumph of the gods,
These gods without flesh nor blood,
These gods that laugh sadistically
At the bite of the stained blade,
The blade that bites the marked entrails.

Ha! This ceremony!
The ceremony that carries away
The silence of the looming day.

How much more strident screaming
Does the merciless god need to hear?
How much more untarnished blood
Does the vampire-god need to quench his thirst?
How many more scraps of flesh
Does the lazy god need to satisfy his stomach?
How many more acid tears streaming
Down these innocent and guilty faces
Does the god who hates agriculture and loves alcohol need?

The girls are indeed guilty and hostage to a culture that has long run out of breath. They are guilty enough to be born daughters of the gods. The ravaging blade in their tender flesh rends the apparent harmony of this morning's tune with the complicity and sarcastic laughs of awe-inspiring sarcophaguses and worm-eaten vampires, creatures of an invisible fertility and abundance only seen by Jakuni through the faceless mask of their dying culture as its ultimate defenders cling to its rituals under the uncomprehending gaze of the West.

Out of the ten candidates, one succumbed to the voraciousness of the unforgiving blade.

"It is proof that the gods are not greedy. A single victim offered in sacrifice for the salvation of the clan! That is surely not very costly."

"Your sister has died. It was the will of the ancestors. You, the survivors, are now ready to found your own households. May the gods watch over you and your future families!"

While pronouncing these words, the 'experts' begin to apply kaolin make-up, the kaolin of victory, the victory of honour over the definition of disgrace in Jakuniland.

The girls' hips are covered with a fabric made out of tree-bark. One of the octogenarians anoints each body with sticky karate butter while murmuring the usual incomprehensible words. Day has just broken. Soon the girls set out in single file, an impressive queue followed by their instructors. They exit the forest with the feel of the vicious bite of the blade still in their flesh. Their motion is as slow as the first steps of a baby crab. They march towards the public square of the hamlet. One of them starts singing the song of the 'newborn daughters'. The chorus is taken up by the time-ravaged voices of the instructors. Traditional dances are performed, and drinks served until not one sober man is to be found in the clan. The gods are offered the fruit of abundance occasioned in the course of the year – frogs, lizards, cane rats, snakes and slaughtered goats.

Only a true Jakuni can understand this culture. In colonial times, the French tried unsuccessfully to explain that the water collected from the mountains and the streams was low in iodine content and its exclusive consumption could cause goitre. The Jakuni replied that goitre was a sign of the gods' blessing. As a result, this infirmity soon became a criterion of beauty in the community. The French tried to teach them that soap could prevent skin diseases, but they wouldn't listen. On the contrary, the scabies that covers the body of many Jakunis came to be considered an aspect of stylishness. Whoever had a squint was venerated. Such a person was believed to be able to see in all directions and have a predisposition towards occult vision. If, by the favor of the gods, a young woman could be circumcised and bent-backed, and have patches of scabies with a squint and goiter, her chances of marrying the spiritual chief of the community would be immense.

The ceremony reaches its conclusion; and if by chance the rain falls, this is taken as evidence that the gods are satisfied and are ready to grant special wishes to the people. Some will ask for the power to conquer their enemies, some for favors in politics; there is always a ceaseless stream of selfish petitions.

Then the octogenarians, who had confiscated all the fetishes and the black magic of the earth, offer, on special recommendation, amulets to attract the sympathy of a boss at work, unstoppable poisons to kill rivals or a 'magical padlock' to imprison the soul of anyone who dares challenge them.

The Apostolic and National Redemption Party

"All extreme opinions consume themselves."
Marty Rubin

Previously involved in mysticism, Charles Yassa had now converted to an orthodox form of Christianity. And from this time he had started a massive national crusade to denounce mysticism and all other religions besides apostolic Christianity. He predicted in all papers that the Lord would one day come to Ivory Coast and entrust him with the destiny of the Nation. He would then be able to crush Satan and the religions that were leading the country to hell. In Ivory Coast, very few people considered Charles Yassa a sane man although some said he was an extraordinary fellow and some said he was anointed. But over the years, the president Dieudonné Baziana and his entourage believed that Yassa's mental health was seriously deteriorating. Yassa claimed to have been having supper with Beelzebub, Satan's lieutenant, when he was a member of a mystical school. That is how he learned that mysticism equals Satanism. Sometimes he claimed to have been a security guard in Hell; on other occasions he would say he used to be a cook in that fiery region. But apart from the fundamentalists in his community, for whom Yassa was undoubtedly the delegate of Christ in Abidjan, no one really believed his tales. And so, despite showing an interest in politics with the intention of preparing the Lord's government in Ivory Coast, Yassa had not been able to impose himself as a politician on a national scale.

He was sometimes pastor, sometimes president of a party, sometimes a powerful businessman at the service of Christ. But his capacity to mobilize in Abidjan (where he has an important following) was real. He openly presented himself as the first antagonist of president Baziana, whom he claimed to have seen in a revelation at Satan's dinner table.

"Baziana is the son of Satan," he would say. "We know each other. That's why he refuses to meet me. I promised to exorcise him but he has always refused to be delivered from Satan's claws. He is still eating at the devil's table, gobbling up the direst iniquity. But the Lord will soon floor him and give me political power."

The day following this and other loud outbursts, the newspapers would run headlines such as "Baziana is a Satanist," "Baziana sells Ivory Coast to Satan," "Baziana, son of Satan," "Baziana sleeps with a demon."

François Gavana leader of the opposition socialist party knew that Yassa was an obscure fundamentalist but began to think that his capacity for mobilization against the president could serve his own cause. He also reckoned that a tactical alliance with the Revolutionary Rally of the Northerners could be exploited.

*

Gavana, accompanied by two of his press attachés who were journalists at the daily newspaper *The Direct*, was walking up the endless stairs in front of the temple-congress palace, headquarters of the Apostolic Party of Charles Yassa. Their attention was attracted by the monumental notice board planted in front of the massive building. They stopped and took a closer look at the gigantic board on which was inscribed this invitation:

Come Quench Your Thirst and Restore Your Soul!
Sunday: From 7am to 12am
Political mass against the doings of Baziana, the Beast of the Revelation
Monday: From 7pm – Gifts to the Lord
Tuesday: From 7pm – Concrete illustrated Bible Study
Wednesday: From 7pm – Mass of deliverance and the very final
sabotage of Satan's doings.
Thursday: From 8am to 10pm – Mass for possessed children
Friday: From 7pm – Mass for the real preparation of Ivory Coast, the
New Jerusalem.
Saturday: From 6pm to 11pm: Spiritual cleansing of the newly
converted

François Gavana smiled and shook his head. His press attachés could hardly hide their mocking laughter. How could they believe a single word on this notice board? The pastor was, as always, trying to attract attention. They had come to benefit from his capacity for mobilization. What did it matter that his followers believed that Charles Yassa was anointed! And so they ignored the fact that there was a long history behind the creation of his Church and political party. Indeed, the building of this community had not been as easy as one would imagine. His very followers were discouraged by Satan when Yassa revealed that Abidjan had been chosen by the Lord to be the New Jerusalem. They couldn't swallow such an astonishing revelation but, quickly inspired by the Lord, Yassa would have the bright idea of sharing some of his responsibilities with his followers. Most men like power and responsibilities; they like to be in charge of someone to highlight their importance. And so members who were hardly in the community for more than a month started to be involved in the daily life of the Church-political party; in this way Yassa won his first real victory over Satan.

He divided the community into five major departments; all departments were to work in collaboration. Yassa said it was the most efficient way to corner and floor the enemy; Satan being very clever, only an efficient strategy could subjugate him. And he taught his followers to always act with anticipation – that's the only way to counter and floor the devil. For more specialized advice he created the *Department of Anticipated Actions and Detection of the Evil Spirit*. Most people have one thing in common: they are weak. So to prevent followers from going back to Satan after their conversion, the *Department of Post-Conversion Consolidation* was created. This division was to work very closely with a third, named *Department of the Lord's Oracles*. This last division was the only one permitted to prophesize during the mass-meetings conducted by the pastor. If Satan appears powerful, it is simply because he does not work alone; he has numerous colleagues and disciples to back him up. Therefore the reverend pastor decided to implement a similar team called the *Spiritual Commando for the Apocalypse and the final Assault against Satan*. Finally, to prevent the members of the community from falling into sexual temptation, the *Department of Spiritual Watch and Moral Discipline* was invented. The members of this last department were to always write down on a pad any suspicious behavior of their fellows. Who is in their company? Are they gossiping? Are they decently dressed? Are they over-eating in times of penitence? Are they frequenting bars? These were just a small sample of areas of conduct to be monitored.

All departments were to meet every Saturday and conduct the mass for cleansing the newly converted. Yassa recorded the names and addresses of all members in a copy book entitled, 'The Book of the Elected'. In order to constantly activate the flame of the Lord, some parishioners voluntarily decided to keep vigil at the temple-congress palace. For many days and nights they would give thanks and offer praises to the Lord. Some would fast for months. Doesn't the Bible say, "Happy are those who are thirsty and hungry for they shall be satisfied in heaven?" This hardcore had found their way to the Lord so why should they undergo any training scheme and apply for a job? Why should they further their studies, sharpen their brains and become erudite if everything good in the hereafter was going to be theirs? They understood that life on earth is temporal, vain. They were poor but their hearts had been comforted; with their discipline they had managed to break the chains of daily bondage and stress, which in truth are generated by the human obsession to plan our own lives. They had made a decision to ask God to be in charge of their destiny. And if at the end they died poor, heaven would be their destiny – for is it not the Grace of God to be poor since "it's easier for a camel to get through the hole of a needle than it is for the rich to go to heaven?" Glory to God to have guaranteed the Afterlife for the poor!

The greedy and the possessed see poverty as a divine curse; that is why they blaspheme. Those who live in cupidity see in wealth their own heaven on earth. They ignore the fact that life on earth is 'wind harvesting'. For as Yassa said, "When, in His glory, the Lord shall return on golden clouds, those who wasted their time working and collecting wealth will realize their stupidity. Yes, watch out! Do not think that the Sunday church collections are the fruits of men's hard work. No, they are not! Gold and silver belong to God, owner of everything. He only gets back what is due to Him for the fulfillment of His work."

Of course, some evil and jealous people, possessed by the spirit of contestation and criticism, think that it is wrong to use the workers' donations to feed the parishioners, forgetting that the most zealous members of Yassa's community are the unemployed. But where else should they get the financial means to feed themselves and be able to travel and spread the gospel? Tragically, the unbelievers do not come to understand that, if it is useless to work, given the imminent return of the Lord, it is not a sin to use the workers' donation to accomplish the Lord's mission. Poor doubting souls who cannot understand the secret of life and thus get agitated! Possessed and made foolish by Satan, deep understanding is out of their reach. Does the Holy Bible not declare in Proverbs 24-7, that "Wisdom is too high for the madman?" And to make matters worse, these are cowards who have never dared open the Bible?

Pastor Yassa was always inspired by the Lord. Having a clear knowledge of the doings of Satan and his disciples, he acted preemptively to muzzle them. For instance, he took various precautions regarding the Parishioners way of dressing. He knew that the lay members would think that the community used the donations to dress its members. For example, the females would always carry a veil on their heads. Not even one would be seen without as they might seduce the Unbeliever. Yassa would repeat that the veil was supremely important for female Christians. It was the sign through which the angels would recognize the 'Daughters of the Lord' on the day of glory. And since the Angels might come while a Sister in Christ would perhaps be under the shower, the reverend suggested that the veil be hung on the exterior handle of the bathroom door. In doing so, the Angels would realize that beyond the bathroom door, a faithful servant of the Lord was waiting. They would then be able to identify the Sister and take her away to heaven.

With regard to everyday dress, skirts should fall to the ankles to prevent the spirit of sex from seeing a single part of the legs that could drive men to fantasy. Yassa prohibited any form of modern make-up. The application of any beauty powder, perfume or other beauty cream used by 'the girls of this world' or 'Baziana's bitches' were similarly banned. If a walking pagan man was getting close, the Sisters in Christ should look away in the opposite direction. If there was another man in the opposite direction, the girls should moreover, bow their heads. For Satan is very clever. One must be ever vigilant. The males in the community were also to dress decently. They should wear long sleeved shirts, buttoned up to the neck to prevent the sisters of the community from falling into sexual temptation.

However, in spite of all these precautions, jealous people 'possessed' by the spirit of gossiping still had something to say. Indeed, when the community later bought its own bus and some musical instruments for glorifying the name of the Lord, unbelievers got embittered. They did not forgive the pastor for having moved from his shantytown to the French Riviera (where most executives in Abidjan lived). They couldn't handle their bitterness when one morning the pastor parked his brand-new Porsche Cayenne in front of the church.

In reality, the lifestyle of the pastor had changed. Those who still doubted the Lord simply had not yet seen the new Charles Yassa. In the temple-congress palace of the apostolic church and political party, he was wearing a purple *galero*, garnished with five red tassels. His golden robe was unfolded to his bright-red moccasins. A maroon ribbon with three crosses hung from his waist. On his little finger was a massive golden ring marked with a bold crucifix. During the mass-meetings, one of his disciples sitting behind him would fan the pastor despite the electric fan standing at his left.

Now only the ignoramus and the possessed still do not believe in the Lord. They do not know that God's servant should not live in misery; for the Lord's shadow constantly surrounds him. If most community members are still struggling in life, it is because they are not righteous, are still possessed like the unbelievers. Tired of suffering their frustration, they had decided to infiltrate Yassa's holy community and spoil it from within. Ha! Yassa truly suffered.

Indeed, one evening in the course of the *Mass of Deliverance and Very Final Sabotage of Satan's Doings*, an Oracle of the Lord nearly had a fight with a pagan possessed by the spirit of espionage who had infiltrated the church. The spy was later identified as an agent of the president, Dieudonné Baziana. In his prophesy, the oracle that day proclaimed, "Here are the words of the Lord! There is among us someone possessed by the spirit of alcohol. He is wearing a yellow dotted shirt and red trousers. He is light in complexion. His height is a hundred and seventy centimeters. He leaves in Bellville. He is married and has two kids. I, the Lord, saw him in the company of pagans drinking beer yesterday. If the described brother hears my words, and shows humility, I, the Lord, will forgive him."

As soon as the oracle's prophecy ended, a male matching the description stood up.

"My Lord," he said, "it is true. I was drinking beer yesterday in the company of unbelievers. But your Oracle who has just spoken was with me in that bar."

The oracle who was facing the assembly then screamed, "Liar! You're a blasted liar!"

But the spy calmly replied, "No, I am not. We were together. I beg you to not deny this. Please."

A noisy discussion then started between both men. A murmur of indignation contaminated the assembly. Had it not been for the wise intervention of Yassa, a worse scenario would have happened. Yassa ordered the man possessed by the spirit of alcohol and a spy of the president Baziana to sit down. The Oracle was then asked to carry on with the prophecies.

"I am the Lord God of Abraham, God of Jacob. If someone hears my voice, he should act accordingly. If not, my anger will be implacable. You, Ho, you, Lady Imbua, I am your Lord. I am talking to you. Give your piano to my church. My children need your piano to sing my holy name. Do not be selfish my daughter, give your piano to my church. These are the words of the lord."

Subsequently a lady stood up from the assembly. She looked confused. Yet she bravely said, "My dear Lord, I heard your call. I desperately want to give this piano to your church. But my Lord, please note that the piano is not mine. It belongs to my younger sister. She recently moved into my house following a quarrel with her husband. I'm keeping some of her belongings. I'm very sorry my Lord, I would have given it to you had it been mine, believe me, my Lord. Thank you, Lord!"

The lady then sat down.

The reverend, most faithful among the faithful ministers of the Lord, never dropped his close collaborators who were themselves sanctified. He concluded that the spirit of division, of selfishness, the mottoes of unbelievers such as Baziana and those who were jealous of his progress and his divine work, was slowly penetrating the community. And to counter such dangerous currents, he then exposed the two cases of the day to the Lord.

"Brothers and sisters, let us close our eyes and pray. "Spirit of contestation, spirit of selfishness, I have removed your masks. I command you to exit this assembly in the Holy name of the Lord! For the Lord's anger will be pitiless towards you! Amen!"

"Amen!" The assembly answered.

Yassa was right! He was always right since the Lord inspired him. He managed to floor the spirit of alcohol; Baziana's spy, who had tried to slander the Oracle, left the community. The spirit of selfishness that the pastor persecuted that day also disappeared; indeed, Lady Imbua came back to the temple-congress palace with the piano. She had convinced her sister that the Lord himself needed it. When the assembly saw the piano, they all started to magnify the name of the Lord for the miracle.

Also that day, a young sister in Christ was weeping ceaselessly. But nobody paid any attention to her while she was crying. Only when she opened her mouth to give out a loud death rattle, did she drew the attention of the assembly. The pastor suspended the benedictions and begged the young lady to move closer to the altar.

"My daughter, what is the matter? Have you lost a close parent?"

The sister shook her head.

"Are you perhaps ill?"

"No", she said, her voice drowned by some shaking sobs.

"Do you have any particular worry? Come now, do not underestimate your Lord. Let him carry your load. Tell me what is going on."

The sister in Christ felt more confident. Yet she bowed her head and said, "Pastor, the... (sniff)...the Lord is marvelous....hiiiiiiii.... booooooo . . ."

She started to cry again.

"Please keep your head," the pastor now took her hand. "Come, my daughter, speak freely and you will be healed."

The sister then calmed down somewhat and added, "The Lord is rea . . . really gooooood. Hiiiiii . . . It's the miracle of the pia . . . pianoo-oooo . . . hiiii . . ."

"Alleluia," said Yassa. "Your faith is endless my daughter."

How proud she was to have witnessed the great miracle performed by the Lord through what is still known in the community as 'The Miracle of the Piano'. The Parishioners, with a single voice, started to sing a hymn to thank the Lord. The entire assembly followed the beat of the drums.

And so Yassa had been through many adversities before he got to his current state of blessedness. How good and pleasant it was to look back and see the crooked road and the long way to the building of his community and political party! Fortunately, he had long left this hectic beginning behind him. And often, when he thought about it, he realized how grateful one should be to the Lord. It was a real victory, the victory of God over Satan and his Delegate, Dieudonné Baziana.

The Protest March 1

*"His supporters will push him to disaster
unless his opponents show where the dangers are."*
Walter Lippmann

François Gavana, leader of the opposition socialist party, and his press attaché decided to meet Yassa. They found the president of the Apostolic Church and political party, reverend-pastor, God-anointed delegate to the Ivory Coast, Charles Yassa and his disciples in the middle of politico-biblical study. As soon as the Reverend President Pastor saw Gavana, he stood up from his delicate, soft sofa and shouted, "Alleluia! God bless you son of Israel, son of Abraham!"

"Amen!" Replied the dozen Yassa followers; mainly members of the *Spiritual Commando for the Apocalypse and the Final Assault against Satan* who were sitting by.

"Thanks reverend, for such a hearty welcome. God bless you," Gavana replied.

The two leaders and Gavana's attachés sat down.

"My dear Gavana, I heard about the satanic arrogance of the security minister regarding your peaceful public protest."

Gavana, a Roman Catholic, was a little moderate. But he knew that at crucial times such as these, one should bury one's own convictions and use a likewise aggressive tone to content the pastor and make him his calculated ally.

"Alleluia! The cancellation of my meeting was a satanic decision indeed."

"Amen! But my dear Gavana, how can the man of God help you today?"

"Well, on Monday I would like all sons and daughters of this country to invade the streets of the CBD to ask President Baziana, the dictator and thief and the ..." Gavana paused, looking for the right words to touch Yassa and his fanatical lieutenants who were attentively following his every word. "How can I say . . . that thief and ..."

"Satanist!" shouted one of Yassa's disciples.

"Yes, the Satanist . . . to leave the presidential palace at once!" re-echoed Gavana.

"You know my dear Gavana, Satan holds this country at ransom. We must kick him out of here. Satan and his agent Baziana must get out! Ha! This Baziana!" Yassa was really disgusted.

"But reverend, I believe that in order to create a more massive movement, we must invite our brothers from the *Revolutionary Rally of the Northeners* as well."

"Keep off Satan! Keep OFF!" roared Yassa as he suddenly stood up. "Never! Ne-ver! The Bible declares that all have sinned and have fallen short of the glory of the Lord. The curate of the Lord mixing with northerners? Muslims? This is a joke my dear Gavana, isn't it?"

Yassa then started to speak the language believed to be that of angels to exorcise the 'satanic words' Gavana had just pronounced: *rococo-rocaca-rocaba-chidada*.

After noting that his last proposal was disturbing the 'tactical alliance', Gavana decided to redeem himself.

"My humble apologies, reverend. But can I count on your support this Monday?"

Yassa stood up once again and turned towards his lieutenants. Smiling broadly, he said, "The Lord has just spoken to him. Alleluia!"

"Amen!" The disciples droaned.

Yassa slowly sat down and murmured to Gavana, "Forget about the northerners, the Muslims and their master Satan, and I will be with you on Monday."

Light shone from Gavana's face – he had the support of the President Reverend Pastor Charles Yassa!

"My dear Gavana," the reverend added as a conclusion, "You should think of giving your life to Jesus. He told me that He loves you. Without Him in your life, you won't achieve much."

Gavana, fearing that any maladjusted answer might change Yassa's mind, kept quiet.

"Do you hear me?" Yassa insisted. "I have to deliver you from Satan's claws."

After a few moments, praying that he was on the right track, Gavana said: "I am already a Christian, reverend. I am a Roman Catholic."

"Jesus Christ!" shouted back Yassa. "Rather be a pagan than a Roman Catholic! Anyway, I will deliver you later. At least for now you accept Jesus in your life."

After these words he stood up. The exchanges were over. Taking his leave, Gavana said, "May God bless you. Of course I will give my life to Jesus."

The following day, the opposition newspaper *The Direct* ran a tactical story on Gavana. Fearing that the information might not be taken seriously if the headline quote was provided by Yassa (who was generally seen as intolerant and crazy), the journalists wrote, 'An anointed man of God pronounces, "Gavana, God loves you!"'

Abidjan held the world record for rumour-mongering. No one knew how supporters of the *Revolutionary Rally of the Northerners*, not invited by Gavana, got the information. They were feverishly getting ready. It was now or never for them to sort out their own cause. How long could they stand to be persecuted for carrying bushy beards and dressing in robes? Baziana's police systematically and carefully checked the papers of any individual sporting a beard – especially one dressed in a long robe; all this while the non-Muslim population went around freely. It was also true that Muslims in the Ivory Coast were not easily distinguishable from citizens of neighbouring Burkina Faso and Mali who were predominantly Muslims. However, the extreme zeal shown by some tribalistic police officers who would systematically ask any man with a beard or dressed in a robe to show his visa or visit permit, had grossly upset the Muslims of the Ivory Coast. When a group of people were walking along the street, the police would let those who did not have a beard pass through while the bearded ones were stopped and questioned for hours. A Muslim could not easily get a certificate of nationality. He needed to provide more than his identification documents. He needed to attach to his application the I.D. book of his parents and grand-parents and prove that he was not from Burkina Faso or Mali. Was it a secret order from the president Baziana? Were the police officers, mostly southerners, over-doing their job?

On this other Monday of December, at 7am, the CBD of Abidjan was experiencing an exceptional atmosphere. There were strident whistles and noisy horns as two thousand marchers headed by François Gavana and the famous reverend and president of the *Apostolic Party for the National Redemption*, Charles Yassa, stomped the streets of Abidjan. The two leaders held each other's hand. But they looked surprised after failing to see any police ready to disperse the procession as the minister of public security had promised.

In the streets of the business centre, other crowds were busy with their daily worries. On a sidewalk some tourists were standing, cameras dangling from their necks. At least they took note – and filmed the impressive movement of the marching crowd. Nearby another bunch of strollers went about preoccupied with their usual exchanges. Meanwhile the marchers started singing some local songs and headed towards Republic Square where Gavana and Yassa would shortly address the crowd. Still there were no police forces around.

Soon Republic Square was fully packed. Around the large plank-made platform, where Gavana and Yassa were standing hand in hand, were some large and vivid banners.

Where is press freedom? Baziana must resign. Gavana for president. Boss Baziana's whore gets fucked in a bar. Baziana = billionaire. No more Misery for Ivorians! No to the Hegemony of Baziana's tribe!

Gavana, to whom someone handed a loudspeaker, opened the show.

"My hearty greetings to the brothers and sisters of the Apostolic Party!"

A thunder-like applause erupted from the crowd.

"Alleluia! Amen! "

"I greet the tireless freedom fighters of the Socialist Party!"

"Viva! Viva!"

"Comrades, we are sick and tired!"

"Sick and tired! Sick and tired!! Sick and tired!"

The crowd turned the expression of his anger into a chorus. They were fully behind him! He lifted up his right hand, waiting for the euphoria to cool off before carrying on.

"Comrades, we are here at this very place where just a few years ago our hero, Andrew Mane, was murdered!"

"Baziana murderer! Baziana murderer!!"

"Are we ready to face his guns?"

"Baziana must resign! Baziana must resign!!"

"Comrades, once we are done here, we will pay a visit to Baziana. He should give us the keys of the presidential palace. He should hand them over . . . today!"

"Baziana, dictator! Baziana, dictator!! "

"Can you allow thieves to rule you?"

"No thief, no! Baziana burglar!"

"Can you accept bitches to rule you?"

"Arleta, Baziana prostitute!Arleta prostitute!!"

After several more venomous invectives against Baziana and his spouse Arleta, Gavana passed the microphone to Christ's delegate in Ivory Coast. When President Reverend Pastor Yassa took the relay, excitement was at fever pitch.

"Alleluia!! Glory to the God of Abraham!! God of Israel!!"

"Amen!! Alleluia!!"

"Brothers and sisters, the time has come for our Lord's glory!"

"Amen! Alleluia!!"

"The Devil is cornered like a rat. No escape is possible at this stage!"

"Alleluia!!"

"Satan, and his disciple, Baziana, will be defeated!"

Then Yassa and his devotees started singing a combat chorus.

"Higher, higher, higher!"

"Jesus is higher!"

"Lower, lower, lower!"

"Satan is lower!"

"Higher . . . higher ..."

Finally Yassa yelled, "Brothers and sisters, let us pray for the immediate downfall of the Devil and his agent Baziana. Let us all close our eyes and pray."

The whole crowd, pagans in the ranks of Gavana included, took a praying position. At such moments it is not a bad idea to compromise. Anything likely to facilitate the collapse of Baziana could not be neglected – one never knows where the divine grace that could make him bite the dust could come from. Now Baziana was a son of the Baule ethnic group who thought themselves superior; they were the richest farmers in the land. Did this make them the only group whose members qualified to become president? Enough was enough! The demonstrators bowed down their heads to pray for the immediate end to this injustice.

"Brothers and sisters, I said close your eyes. I know some of you still have your eyes open."

Yassa was really anointed. How else could he tell some eyes were still open when his own were already closed?

"Lord," he started, "Your children are here. They are asking you to remember the promise you made. Give them the political power to enable your Mighty Name to be glorified. You promised to floor Satan and his agent Baziana. Talk to your people now! Talk to them – abata-cococorida-cocoshiba-rabatacacasha! Alleluia?!"

The prayer was accompanied by powerful applause. It seemed to François Gavana, who stood behind Yassa, that the pastor imagined he was in his temple. The crowd saw him whispering something into the pastor's ears.

Yassa suddenly turned to the crowd and screamed, "To the presidential palace! All of us! Now!"

And he marched down from the podium and began walking towards the palace which was only five hundred metres away. As one person, the huge crowd started to follow him.

Unlike the Republic Square where everyone could casually take a walk and kill time, the security round the presidential palace was formal and tight. The republican guards, armed with automatic assault guns, ringed the massive building. In front of them, the wire mesh beyond the gate made a significant barricade. The front entrance was heavily guarded but the presence of the soldiers did not seem to intimidate Gavana, Yassa and their militants.

Soon those in front pushed their way towards the colossal gate. They were promptly challenged as one of the guards commanded them to HALT! Gavana cleared a way through the dense crowd. In a few moments he was at the gate. He was sweating copiously. He drew a face towel from a pocket, wiped his sweaty forehead and bushy armpits. And after he had blown his nose into the face towel, he delicately put it back into his pocket and said to the standing guard, "We are here to see Baziana."

"Who the hell is Baziana?"

Gavana could see the soldier laugh and touch his gun handle.

"You don't know Baziana? Dieudonné Baziana – the so called president of Ivory Coast."

"And what makes you think I should?"

Meanwhile the crowd had flooded all over Republic Square and now started to chant.

"Here to meet Baziana! Here to meet Baziana!"

"You don't know Baziana? You don't know the fool you're guarding?"

The soldier was now silent as the opposition leader became more vocal.

"If you don't know the criminal you're guarding, then I can guess what's inside your skull."

"And what is inside my skull?"

"Cotton, pure cotton – not a single piece of brain. Open this gate right now. We must speak to Baziana at once!"

Two meters separated Gavana and the soldier standing behind the massive wire mesh gate. The soldier pretended not to have heard Gavana's sarcastic words and came closer to the gate. He looked amused and used a pleasant tone full of those diversions known only to an expert republican soldier.

"I beg your pardon, sir."

Gavana literally screamed at the soldier.

"Listen carefully this time! I said if you don't know Dieudonné Baziana, the thief, then you are not . . ."

He was not allowed to complete his insult. A violent and burning gun butt struck his jaws sending him meters away from the gate. He did not collapse immediately thanks to the militants massed behind him but streams of blood flowed down his mouth. His four front incisors crushed by the butt fell out of his mouth. His chest was red with blood. Who can handle such pain? He collapsed. Two militants quickly dragged the leader of the Socialist Party along the rough asphalt away from the scene.

The soldier at the other side of the gate walked back cautiously.

Someone shouted from the crowd, "Gavana has been killed! Gavana is dead! Ambulance, ambulance!"

Gavana seemed to have completely lost consciousness when he was carted away. But the Reverend Yassa rose to the occasion. Lifting up his right hand, he called on the crowd to retreat. Then the militants picked up some sizeable stones from the side-street and, as they retreated, pelted them at the windows of the downtown skyscrapers and luxury fashion shops. Their fury was unquenchable. Hawkers, tourists and passersby scampered in all directions. Drivers hooted chaotically. Interminable traffic jams quickly formed along several streets as cars sped out of the business centre.

Then the police arrived. Strident sirens aggravated the panic as well as their throwing tear gas canisters in all directions. The street sellers packed up whatever they could and fled amid the general confusion. Alerted, all cab and bus drivers abruptly modified their schedules, and in less than fifteen minutes there was no public transport at the militants' disposable. Taunted and surrounded by the police, they capitulated en masse. But the police were merciless and the disorder was indescribable. Those severely injured and unable to run or escape the force's fury lay on the ground as a sign of surrender. The only happy people about were the looters whose task was eased by the general confusion. The police arrested dozens of protesters among whom was the Honourable Reverend President Pastor Charles Yassa.

Two police officers held the reverend by the collar of his shirt and dragged him off. Then they sat him on the ground, and grouped in a semi-circle, pitilessly thrashed the man of God. Their captive bled abundantly from the mouth, his left eye closed up. Yassa lost consciousness. One of the officers, turning towards the captives packed in the back of a police van, shouted:

"You'll get your share, sons of dickless!"

An officer jumped into the van, struck out with his bludgeon, breaking a couple of ribs and heads while pushing back the already crammed militants to create space for the pastor. Then he grabbed Yassa and brutally threw him inside.

The vans, full of captives drove off towards the central police station.

The following day, the 'title readers' of Abidjan or titologists (those who never read further than the newspaper headlines) gathered in front of the city's newsstands to get a general picture of what had transpired. Front pages were blazoned with headlines like: Gavana in coma; Gavana almost dead; Gavana is dead; Yassa: the Man of God is with his Maker; Baziana challenges the Almighty.

It was three o'clock. The whole of Abidjan had moved to the city center where the justice court was under unusual surveillance. Since dawn the police had encircled the entire CBD to prevent Gavana and Yassa's sympathisers from protesting what they suspected would be a parody of a trial.

The severity of the fifty years old, bald judge, Samuel Nogo, was a well-established fact. 'The Opposition Crusher', as they called him, entered the justice courtroom an hour later than scheduled. He spent an additional thirty minutes murmuring an inaudible speech to the public prosecutor sitting at his right. He threw a bemused glance at the defendants, numbering about a hundred, massed in front of him. A throng of Yassa's comrades had turned up to attend the session. But from the gallery where they sat, they could not even see their leader, whose left eye was covered by a leaking yellowish plaster.

In most politically motivated crimes of vandalism, very few magistrates in Ivory Coast followed the official procedures; the outcome of the trial being known to all in advance. The judge seemed ready to ensure that the current one was no exception.

"So that's it," he said, addressing himself to the defendants gathered in front of him. The contemptuous look in his eyes betrayed his eagerness to mete expeditious justice. "The snake," he carried on, "is biting its own tail."

"Boss," said a perfectly illiterate accused from the *Revolutionary Rally of the Northerners* before being invited to. "Boss, I am done no crime ever."

"Is that right?" the judge replied. "You did not commit any crime, you say? Please tell me, sir, who broke into the shops? Who burned down the car dealerships? Who attacked the police forces?"

"Boss, we was peaceful. I don't know nothing about breaking shops and burning what-what. I know nothing."

"That is so true, you really know nothing at all." In a more serious tone the judge carried on. "Did you know your public protest was illegal, not authorized?"

"Not knowing."

"You did not? Why were you marching anyway?"

"I am march from Ottala."

"Oh, yes, of course, for Dr Ottala. And what is your name, dear sir?"

"My calling is Musa Sula."

"Please bear with me while I consult your file". The judge then began to flip through the files slowly. "Sula, you said?"

"Yes boss."

"Here we go. *Musa Sula, country of origin: Burkina Faso. Born 1967; Unmarried, father of three kids.* Is that correct?"

"Yes boss."

The judge who was reading the file turned back to his interlocutor and proceeded.

"And what was our friendly Burkinabe citizen doing in a protest march intended for the citizens of this country?"

"I born in Ivory Coast."

"I know, it is clearly mentioned in your file. You were indeed born in Ivory Coast."

"I am work for Ivory Coast. My dad, my mom is work for Ivory Coast always long before."

The judge slowly pulled his spectacles down to the tip of his nose. "So?"

"So my kids is born to Ivory Coast."

"What is your point?"

The defendant smiled. "

"So I march. The protest bring good to Ivory Coast."

"Do you know that foreigners are not allowed to practice politics in this country?"

"I not be a foreigner. I born, all my kids born, to Ivory Coast."

The judge took a deep breath so as to suppress the urge to laugh at the supreme ignorance of his interlocutor.

"So, since the gentleman is born and has been working in Ivory Coast, he is a citizen of this country. Is that correct? And he has full rights to do politics in this country?"

"Yes, boss," the accused said with assurance.

The judge held his chin, looked at the accused and shook his head once more. He knew that most foreigners sympathised with the *Revolutionary Rally of the Northerners* because they believed it was only a matter of time before Baziana's administration would deport them to their country of origin. Indeed, did Baziana not suspect all northerners of being foreigners?

He sighed before continuing, "That's so strange."

"I say to you Mr. Judge, sir, I am not stranger," shot back the accused, Musa Sula.

The judge was not surprised. It was well known that the foreigners born in Ivory Coast were numerous and generally ignored the fact that they could be issued citizenship on simple request once they clocked sixteen years of residence. He also knew that most foreigners were illiterate and believed that Dr Hassan Ottala, the *Northerners* leader, would immediately grant them citizenship upon assuming the presidency.

The judge then proceeded, "Who else is innocent?" While waiting for an answer, he saw someone in the crowd murmuring to himself as if praying.

"My goodness, who do I see there – the son of God himself? Pastor Yassa! What do you have to say for yourself? I was told you refused any attorney's assistance. Pastor, what do you have to say for yourself?"

All the accused turned to the Pastor who was still deep in prayer.

"Please say something," someone in the crowd begged.

Then suddenly President Reverend Pastor Yassa shouted through clenched jaws, "O Lord, all have sinned and shall be deprived of Your glory! 'I punish fathers' iniquity till the last generation! The revenge is mine! Vanity of vanity, all is vanity! Nations fooled me, but the stone that the builder refused turned out to be the cornerstone! No one is righteous on earth!' Rabata-chococo Ripaparipopotipotipatipo . . . Alleluia!"

"Amen!" Answered the militants standing next to him.

The judge looked at the public prosecutor who did not seem to understand the pastor's plea. In a low voice he asked the prosecutor whether he thought the pastor was mentally ill.

"I doubt that," the public prosecutor said.

"Is that all, reverend?"

Yassa remained silent, his head bowed as he was still deep in prayer.

"Pastor?" The judge tried once more.

The Pastor then, pointing his finger at the judge, shouted, "You are the Devil, I recognise you! Out of here! Get out of there! Your fate is sealed, Satan! Shut your big mouth, Beelzebub! Show me your hands! Put them up! Up, up! If not, I'll send you back to the desert where you belong. Surrender now, Satan! Rococo richadadatipa tipatipotipo."

A deep cathedral silence descended over the Palace of Justice. Did the judge think this was a dream? He only knew Yassa through the press; this was his first face-to-face encounter.

A few minutes later the public prosecutor, bored with Yassa's gibberish, read out the incriminating charges and, without giving the accused the opportunity to defend themselves individually, Judge Noko promptly confirmed their collective guilt with respect to vandalism, making a public nuisance and aggression towards the state police. He then handed down a blanket sentence: three years imprisonment and a fine of 500 000 CFA.

Pleased with his day's work, the prosecutor sat down smiling.

"Thank you, Your Honour. This most important matter is now closed."

The Protest March 2

People sleep peaceably in their beds at night only because rough men stand ready to do violence on their behalf.

George Orwell

François Gavana, his wife and children at his bedside, was still in hospital recovering from his injuries. At first his gums were swollen and his lips sewn up so that during the first week of hospitalization, he had not been able to utter a single word. But now, two weeks later, he began to regain his usual spirits for he still felt determined to knock down Baziana. His political advisers, who came to comfort him, had several excellent propositions. One of them, Séverin Kolo, suggested it would be wise to attract the attention of the international community.

"Alone," he said, "we won't achieve much against Baziana."

"That's true," Gavana replied. "But weren't we supposed to use our next weapon . . . the strike at the University?"

"Yes, but that can wait for a while."

"Till when?"

"I beg you not to worry about that. Think of those who finance Baziana, think of those who give him the money that keeps him in power."

"I don't follow you. Be more precise."

"Think of France, of America, of England. Think of messing up his collaboration with the superpowers. Believe me, once they disavow Baziana, the people of Ivory Coast will turn to us."

Gavana, still doubtful, asked, "What if they don't disavow him? Baziana and his Baule brothers have been looting this country for so long and it suits your French, English and American friends. That's why they say nothing."

"That's true."

"So why should they react now?"

"Because we will ask them to."

Gavana laughed bitterly. "Because we ask them ..."

"Look, we are here with a photographer. He will ..."

"Take a picture of me in bed? Come now, that won't work. Beside

I am almost fine."

The head of the Socialist Party was expecting something more shocking, something more likely to compromise or humiliate Baziana. Was he not dreaming of an 'historical' revenge after what the republican guard of Baziana had done to him?

But the advisor was bent on pushing on with his plan. He knew that if Gavana would let him speak further, he would be able to convince him.

"Gavana," he said. "Please listen, you might just find yourself interested."

"Well, I am listening."

The counsellor made a sign with his finger. The photographer sitting next to the entrance stood up. From his bag, he pulled out a camera and a big chain. The chain was made of some heavy steel links like those fastened around the necks of Negroes during the slave trade. The photographer also took out an official uniform of the presidential guard, with a truncheon.

Gavana still did not understand.

"And then?" he asked impatiently. "What is this?"

The counsellor simply smiled before offering an explanation.

"Great!" he said. "So, here we are. We put these chains around your neck, your armpits and your ankles . . . a voluminous bandage on your mouth, stained with a few drops of red ink, that will do for the missing blood . . . someone wearing the republican guard uniform, stands by your bedside displaying a terrible mood, and plays the watching guard with a machete dangling from his belt. And click! The camera flashes. The picture tours America, France, the U.K. The impact will simply be unstoppable! How's that?"

Gavana almost fell from the bed where he was lying as he shouted, "That's marvellous! You are a genius, Séverin! That's exactly what we need. But something is still missing in this picture."

"What can that be?" the counsellor asked.

"There is no weapon for the one who plays the republican guard. All Baziana's guards carry weapons; their absence will make people doubt the photos' credibility."

"I thought about it. But remember the opposition is currently under strict surveillance. It's too risky to drive around with a gun at this time. We can clone a gun to the picture using the computer."

Gavana was visibly joyful.

"Séverin, you are my lifetime brother! Let's do it now."

It was almost 10 a.m. The curious crowd, as always, had gathered round the busiest newsstand in 'Soweto', the most miserable shantytown of Abidjan, to peruse the headlines on the dailies. These avid readers of headlines had that morning gathered in a greater number than usual for all opposition newspapers had published on their front page the disturbing picture of François Gavana, with such sensational titles as *Baziana the new slave driver*; *Gavana caged by Baziana*; *Baziana resurrects slavery*; *Gavana in a neo-Nazi concentration camp.*

"No, I can't believe this," one bystander said. "Do you guys see how Baziana treats the opposition?"

"Worse than farm animals," said another.

"This is totally unacceptable," the first bystander said. "Look at this picture. Is this the way to treat a human being?"

"I think the people should show Baziana and his friends that they are not indispensable to this country. On the contrary, they are the very obstacles to true democracy in Ivory Coast."

"I don't agree," another person in the crowd cut in.

"Why not?" Someone else said.

"Because anyone who plays the bad sheep needs a tough shepherd to lead him! Human rights are for humans only! No animal needs human rights! What democracy can Baziana install amid a bunch of animals and vandals?"

"Who is a vandal? The vandals are the police and the members of Baziana's party who infiltrated our march."

"Liar!"

"Yes, I may be a liar but surely not a slave driver!"

"The wages of vandalism is jail! Well done Baziana!"

"My brother, I can see you are a Baule from the president's village and surely a member of the Democratic Party ..."

"Of course, so what?"

"So I say only thieves mingle with thieves. You are certainly a thief!"

"How about you? Your twisted western accent marinated with some stupid socialism stinks like shit!"

"Yes I'm from the west, and I support Gavana who is a son of our region, but I am not a thief!"

"I tell you what, you and your loony Gavana, you are not good enough to wipe the ass of Baziana! Gavana is dirty! He blows his nose at every street corner. He'll never be president as long as we are in this country!"

This last insult was greeted with laughter from the sympathizers of Baziana and the Democratic Party while enraging the socialist who shouted out, "I advise you to talk about Gavana using another tone, you donkey! I never take too long to crush the big mouths of idiots like yourself!"

"Who's an idiot? Your fucken mother or your stupid father?"

The mockers found this funny and laughed their heads off at the expense of Gavana's loyalist.

"Be careful. I warned you. Do you hear me?"

"Please go home, take a shower and there, fuck yourself!"

Before anyone had time to react, the socialist jumped into the crowd and punched Baziana's supporter hard in the face. The man collapsed to the ground, his lips dripping with blood. The crowd of onlookers became more agitated. Upon realising what was happening, more sympathisers of the Democratic Party gathered around. Then more socialists came to give a hand. The wrangle between the parties escalated. Stones were thrown and the wooden news-stand was broken up and turned into weapons. The papers were torn into shreds and scattered all over. Suddenly a siren announced the arrival of the police and the crowd fled in every direction through the alleys of the labyrinth that was the shantytown. That day, neither Baziana, who was surely relaxing at home while sipping some divine nectar, nor Gavana who was still recovering in hospital, knew that a fanatical crowd in this squatter camp was fighting over them.

The following day, the opposition papers headlined: *Baziana Militia Pitiless with Opposition Paper Readers; Press Freedom Abuse: Police Tear Up Opposition Newspapers; Baziana Hates the Poor of Shantytowns.*

"I thought you said Gavana is a free man," President Dieudonné Baziana asked his security minister.

"Yes, of course, Your Excellency," the minister, Gaston Akassu, assured him.

"And this . . . what is this?"

Dieudonné Baziana, ensconced on his favourite couch, grabbed the magazine on the pedestal table close to where he was. On the front page of this famous international paper, which specialised in political scandals, was the disturbing picture of François Gavana wrapped in chains like a Negro in the belly of a slave ship crossing the Atlantic.

"Your Excellency, I am also surprised to see this picture. He's at the Saint Theresa Polyclinic."

Baziana slowly sank even deeper into the comfortable couch and before continuing.

"That's true. The paper confirms it. But why is he chained up in this clinic? Why?"

"Your Excellency, I did not instruct my men to guard him in this hospital, much less ill-treat him."

The minister was completely taken aback by the information. He took a close look at the picture. He was convinced that this was the work of an over-zealous policeman.

The president shook his head some more before posing the one question that had been burning inside him of late.

"Tell me," he said, "have you finally found out who authorised Gavana's protest march? Have you discovered who imitated your voice? You promised to give me the culprit."

"Your Excellency, we are still investiga . . ."

"You have made two mistakes that only begin to make sense in light of the malfunctioning of your team. Would you admit that?"

The minister equated the president's remark with an accusation of serious deception and he knew what the implication was.

"Your Excellency, I request additional time to finalise these two cases; I will shortly be able to solve both."

Baziana, who had all along been talking to his minister without looking at him, now faced him – his expression considerably softer.

"You know what I've been trying to figure out lately, Akassu?" He paused and dropped his voice. "Could there be a spy in our party . . . a spy working for the opposition?"

The minister's face suddenly radiated with life. He had never thought that the extreme vigilance of his team (that had guaranteed his position in several governments) could allow for such mistakes. If he had never doubted the efficiency of his team, he had always suspected a spy in the ranks of the Party. He was even happier that the suggestion had come from the president himself.

"Your Excellency, I must confess I have always suspected that much."

Well, then," the president said. "Why don't you take a good look around and see? I'm sure it will lead to something. And relax, for God's sake. Take some whiskey, some rum?"

"I'll have a few drops of *whiskey*, Your Excellency."

"Help yourself." The president took a sip of the refined Scotch he was drinking. "I hear that Ottala has decided to use the foreigners against us."

"Absolutely, Your Excellency. Quite a number were arrested during the march."

"I thought as much. Very sad how these foreigners are ungrateful ..."

The relaxed atmosphere and the liquor seemed to inspire the minister. He began to talk more freely – though only in acquiescence to everything the president said.

"I've always known these foreigners to be very ungrateful. Still, I can't believe that they, who were born to sell cereals at street corners and keep cattle in the deepest regions of the desert, can do this to Ivory Coast, a country that feeds them. They're nothing but a bunch of simple fishermen and kola nut retailers who take peanuts and tea for dinner in dusty tents. How can they be so unthankful and become politicians! My goodness! And why? Because their stomachs are quite full! And now, *we* are said to be xenophobic! How more wicked and unappreciative can you get?"

The minister spoke with increasing passion which President Dieudonné Baziana quietly put down to the magic effects of the Scotch.

"Your Excellency, we need to contain the foreigners as soon as possible. We should ..."

"Akassu," the President, who was starting to feel bored and tired, called out, "of course we should. Why do you think we are having this discussion? Please investigate those two cases thoroughly and stay alert to every plot in and around the party. I have to rest now. Good night."

And with that, Dieudonné Baziana gulped down the last drop in his glass and slowly closed his eyes.

Baziana on Death Row

If you want total security, go to prison.
There you're fed, clothed, given medical care and so on.
The only thing lacking . . . is freedom.
Dwight D. Eisenhower

The two-meter-wide concrete fence of Abidjan's toughest prison was dispiriting. It reminded one of the mythic walls of China as it disappeared into the depths of the forest located at the Western entrance of Abidjan. To some, the prison was a hell on earth – Abidjan's version of hell. And the facility displayed such great ingenuity that even Satan, along with his apprentices, marveled at this human rival to his domain. Truly, the architects of Abidjan's prison had brought to life an abode that made death a blessing.

A massive conic building hosted the penitentiary administration. Three others were spread out in the vast yard of the prison; these hosted the detainees. One of them, aptly named 'Death Chamber', was alleged to be the final place where certain convicts ended their days. Inside this infamous building, prisoners were kept naked. They were chained and laid on their stomachs or made to sit in pairs with their ankles fastened together. Their genitals and rectal orifices rested in their own wastes, which were infested with maggots and worms. These creatures sometimes crawled over the uncovered backs of the inmates. Since they could not move their legs or arms, the odious and voracious creatures did as they pleased.

In a corner of the 'Chamber', leaning against the wall, was a gigantic, filthy pot that served as a toilet. The 'Chamber' had no window. The inmates, numbering approximately one hundred, hardly saw each other. They all suffered from one kind of respiratory illness or another. Located inside a dense forest, the rate of humidity was exceptionally high. It was hard to distinguish day from night. Some thought they had been jailed for eternity and would almost faint on being told that only six months had elapsed since they had been brought in. Six month! Only frigging six months out of the ten or twenty years of imprisonment to come?

Sometimes, when the cells were exceptionally crowded, and even officials saw this, some inmates would be transferred to upcountry prisons. But it was said that prisoners were executed on their way to the new prisons. Cruel as it may seem, such an unexpected end was far preferable to the treatment they received in the 'Death Chamber', where toxic liquid leaked constantly from the half-meter thick walls. Just one drop of this chemical on a prisoner's skin left ugly inflammations on the skin. Sometimes in the middle of the night, the meowing of a big cat tore through the silence and one of the dying inmates would take his last breathe. The forest was rife with its own psychological terrors and was, in its own way, something of a natural wall that more effectively confined the prisoners. The penitentiary guards on a number of occasions discovered the corpses of those who tried to escape. The corpses had either been torn to shreds or bitten by venomous reptiles. And so no guard bothered to pursue those who tried to escape.

The inmates ate once every two days; and the meal did not contain salt. On this day, two guards were visiting the inmates. It took about ten minutes to unlock the gigantic padlocks and open the cell doors. The process was accompanied by a loud grating noise from the metallic door.

After yanking the door open, one of the sweating guards stepped in with his usual taunt, "My respect to the dead people. Unfortunately, I've some bad news for you. No more food in the kitchen. The State owes too much money to the suppliers. And the suppliers are upset! Can you hear me, in there?"

There was no response.

"Hey, there? Do you hear me from down there? Hey, hooo?"

The echo of the guard's voice reverberated through the vast cell and along the corridor leading up to 'Death Chamber'.

Still there was no response to the guard's gesture.

"Thanks for not answering," he said. "But bear in mind that there is no more food till further notice. Cheers. Ha! Ha! Ha!"

It was not the first time that suppliers had refused to deliver food to the prison nor was it the first time that prisoners were chained together with a rotting body. It was unfortunately impossible for one to kill oneself in this chamber. Visitors, metallic objects and food from outside the penitentiary administration were completely forbidden. Those inmates who were released could not adjust to life in the Ivorian society. Some became blind, or lost their arms or legs. How could such place be called a correctional facility if it could not effect the reintegration of those it purported to have rehabilitated? Despite the multiple calls for improvement from human rights organisations, following distressing testimonies from the survivors of Death Chamber, the various governments did not bother to rectify the situation. Why should anyone be surprised when no member of the government had ever stepped in there?

Unlike in the two other buildings, life in Death Chamber was unbearable. The cell was there . . . far out there, isolated, as if to tell the criminals they were in another world. The second building, five hundred meters away, hosted minors and women. The one closer to the main entrance hosted those who had been convicted of minor offences; life inside was fairer: visitors were allowed. Between these last two buildings and Death Chamber, was a soccer field, a laundry, a kitchen, a mosque and a chapel. Just behind the playground was a bakery. The mouth-watering aroma of baking bread excited the appetite of the inmates. But, of course, no bread was served to any detainee. The aroma formed part of the torture. Moreover, the prison administration was rumored to be selling the bread in town. Yet, officially, all the inmates received three meals a day, including bread for breakfast. The head of the correctional facility would collect money from parents paying visits to their children and pocket it. They even collected donations intended for a number of prisoners who had died long ago.

Charles Yassa, his militants and the members of the Revolutionary Rally of the Northerners were very lucky to be in the building hosting those convicted of minor offences. It was Sunday when Mrs. Gavana and some leaders of the Socialist Party visited the pastor and his co-detainees. They were escorted by a bunch of guards and were informed that Yassa was in the chapel, leading the service. There, they found a very embittered pastor trying to win the attending detainees to his ideology.

"Baziana is dead," he said.

"To hell with Baziana!" The crowd in the chapel shouted in return.

"The Lord will be merciless towards him!" The Pastor said. "May everything that breathes praise the Lord!"

"Amen! To hell with Baziana!"

Most prisoners who were attending the mass were half-starved, skinny, and were dressed in rags. Given the food served in the prison, one could hardly expect anything different. Indeed, the only dish served was nothing but roughly crushed maize porridge with cabbage – boiled in unsalted water. One could often see cockroach-like parasites and a host of other insects floating on the surface. Detainees would not believe that the administration could run out of stock of such horribly infested food that even a starving dog would not touch. It was surely Baziana's fault to have failed to pay the suppliers. He did not care about the poor, the detainees and the sons of God. How can someone who took the finest Parisian champagne at breakfast care about prisoners? It was simply wicked! Baziana must pay it back!

Their bitterness against the system of Baziana had found the necessary yeast for its growth, its expansion: the presence of Charles Yassa. All prisoners were now innocent. It was Baziana's fault that a gangster was locked up in the jail of Abidjan. According to the testimonies following Yassa's mass, no prisoner was rightfully arrested. The corrupted justice of Baziana had jailed the poor rapists, the kind robbers, the gentle crooks and the harmless murderers, who, according to their model of society ought to be set free. Baziana was so wicked. How can he punish a bandit who did everything possible to make sure that no one was hurt in the course of his banditry? A vandal ought not to be arrested. Baziana must pay for being so unjust.

At the end of the purgative mass, Mrs. Sidony Gavana met Pastor Yassa.

"May God be with you!" she said to the pastor.

"Amen!" the later reverted.

"Pastor, would you and your brothers kindly accept these modest presents from our party? And please, continue to pray that peace may return to Ivory Coast. We should ..."

"Mrs. Gavana," Yassa cut in: "May God bless you for your great heart. Believe me, I know the Lord. The only prayer that he'd be pleased to hear now is for the fall of Baziana."

Mrs. Gavana looked frightened by the pastor's prophesy.

"What will happen once Baziana falls?" she asked.

"What will happen? The Lord himself will take over."

"I don't understand," Mrs. Gavana retorted sceptically.

Holding her by the shoulder, the reverend said, "Don't worry about what you don't understand. The Lord will soon overthrow Baziana and He'll entrust to me the destiny of this nation. There will be no more prisons, no more suffering and no more diseases. Even death will run away once the Lord has taken over through his faithful servant."

Mrs. Gavana, who was quietly listening to the Pastor, did not believe a single word; it was all complete nonsense. The Socialist Party only needed Yassa's flocks for public demonstration and other civic and political actions. No one in his right mind ever believed in the arrival of the Lord in Abidjan. That Mrs. Gavana and her friends visited the prison was simply because her husband had asked them to keep in touch with the pastor for the sake of future battles that would pave the way for the Socialist Party's ascendency to power.

But Yassa was adamant that the Lord would give him the power and Gavana relied on Yassa's bunch of followers to marshal popular hatred against Baziana and accelerate his fall. Hassan Ottala and the Muslims planned to discredit Baziana abroad and convince investors to asphyxiate the national economy. Once done, Ottala would re-establish the dignity of the Northerners. In the meantime, the most expedient strategy consisted in hiding one's own conviction and joining hands with those who planned the fall of Baziana. Once Baziana had been dealt with, it would be a matter of sorting out the others. Masks would have to be removed, real faces would be unveiled, new alliances would be formed.

Mrs. Gavana and all the other socialists knew it.

"You are right, reverend. The Lord must kick out Baziana and, at last, give the power to his real children."

In saying the Lord's children, she was in fact thinking of her husband, who was still recovering in hospital. Yassa, in return, interpreted this as a sign of perfect allegiance.

"May God bless you," Yassa said. "Please send my regards to Mr Gavana. Baziana's guards are coming back, our meeting is over. Thanks and take care."

The Vase Tips Over

Neither soldiers nor money can defend a king but only friends won
by good deeds, merit, and honesty.

Sallust

10pm, Saturday, 23 December, province of Akoro. Christmas was just around the corner. Although Christianity is the predominant religion in the south and Islam in the north, the majority of the population are animists. Yet, no one more than an Ivorian indulges in festivities commemorating the birth of Jesus Christ. Throughout the entire holy week the whole country is on leave! People travel to their villages. Civil servants, teachers, shop attendants, factory workers – even the jobless: everybody takes leave. It is a season of sheer merriment. People try to drown their sorrows in alcohol till they can take no more. The festive season is, in fact, the most anticipated week of the year. A wise observer will have noticed that the workers maximise the gaiety of the festive season by planning and going out on most of their endless strikes in the weeks leading up to Christmas. That way, they would end up with almost a month of holidays.

When an Ivorian says that he does not celebrate Christmas, it clearly means that he is depressed. The president, Dieudonné Baziana himself, always returned to his village to celebrate Christmas with his relatives. That evening, he was relaxing after a delightful dinner. The new French advisor, Alan Serge Devaux, who was celebrating Christmas in Ivory Coast for the first time, was in his company. Baziana, custodian of national unity, was thinking about the political crisis that had troubled his country during the past few weeks. True, he had seen more hectic days than the current one – but he was more shaken than he had ever been before. Of course, he trusted that he would overcome the challenge. After all, had he not put his high ranking military officers on maximum alert? A perfectly logical response to his belief that François Gavana and Hassan Ottala, the opposition leaders who were in Paris, were planning something evil. Was it not Gavana who stirred up the students' rage? Was it not the same Gavana instigating the strikers of the central trade union?

Was it not Hassan Ottala who secretly manipulated the Northerners and the international community to sabotage his government's actions?

Dieudonné Baziana knew all this and relied on the army, the police and on his closest generals to protect the nation. He tried to stay serene. No better place than his village, far from Abidjan's noise, to offer tranquility. On Monday, he would go back to his office and carry on with the nation's work in spite of the endless strikes. "They'll surely run out of breath and get back to work," he assured himself – for it was not the first time that people were going on strike or organizing mass protest. However, no matter the length or size of these demonstrations, Baziana never ceased to preside over the country with confidence and inner calm. Devaux, was amazed: Baziana's great serenity had always stunned him. But as they basked in the assurance that all was fine, Baziana received a phone call and sank deeper in the sofa.

"Let me take this call," he said.

"What is happening . . . ?" The Frenchman asked. He wanted to add "Your Excellency," but thought better of it since it would have highlighted his lack of courtesy as more two seconds had already elapsed. But Baziana's mind was far from this gaffe.

"Your Excellency?" Devaux tried to insist once more.

However, the president excused himself, and with an open palm indicated to the advisor not to disrupt the conversation, He rose up on his feet and slowly walked towards the massive bookshelf where some authorized political theories were housed, all the while listening to his caller with rapt attention and forgetting about the Frenchman.

Devaux stood up. He knew that the country was in extreme crisis. He did not need to be told that this late call had some links with recent events; the proof being that Baziana did not switch off his cell phone – he had surely wanted to be reachable at any given time. Suddenly he heard Baziana shouting. Devaux, amazed, was immobile like a robot.

"Calm this down immediately!" the president shouted. "Are you wise to have started the negotiation? . . . When? . . . How much? . . . From one hundred to five hundred thousand C.F.A? This is clearly impossible! Where have you ever seen this? A trooper earning half a million? The State cannot afford this! We are in the midst of an economic re-launch . . . did you tell them? . . . Sorry? But this is an unacceptable blackmail! This is just too crazy! Lock everything! Understood? . . . Is Gilbert with you? (There was a slightly longer pause.) I say, Gilbert . . . Ah, my good

Minister of Economy is with you . . . Great, pass him the phone . . ."

From the other end of the line, Gilbert said, "Hello. Your Excellency?"

"Gilbert, talk with these . . . these youngsters. Tell them we are at the end of the financial year, right? Tell them I'll personally look at their request by the second of January, right?"

"Yes, Your Excellency."

"Explain to them that technically we cannot vote an amendment to the current budget. Tell them!"

The president then cut the conversation and turned back to Devaux.

"Alan, we should perhaps return to Abidjan tonight."

"Is everything okay?"

"I've just spoken to the Defense Minister. The rumors are beginning to take shape."

"What rumor, Your Excellency?" The advisor was also becoming anxious.

"I have just been informed that the troopers of the first Battalion are planning to go on strike tomorrow at dawn. However, the Minister of Defense told me that there's nothing to worry about in his department." The president shook his head in disbelief. "It's so taxing to have to deal with these brainless niggers, Alan. An illiterate negro isn't worth a centime. Believe me; I've done everything for these soldiers. They were just beggars that I recruited to clear the over cluttered streets! Some bus conductors, farm workers, street-corner shoe polishers that I turned into soldiers . . . and this is how they reward me. How ungrateful! Pah!"

Baziana was surprised that the troopers, who had only recently raised a grievance about their uniforms and a missing bulb in their canteen, had turned such requests into a strike. The adviser was also not convinced. Could such minor issues cause the president this much exhaustion?

"Your Excellency, may I please suggest that we get back to Abidjan tomorrow early in the morning."

The president, who was still holding his cell phone, looked at the keypad as if intending to give some urgent orders to his closest generals in Abidjan. Resolutely, he said, "Sorry, we must leave now. I know full well what this is about."

"But Your Excellency . . . it is Christmas," Alan Serge said, not yet convinced that the night journey was necessary.

"Alan," the president responded, "you will soon realise why I should not let you insist."

"Very well, Your Excellency, but please allow me just one question. Are there any superior officers attending the negotiation with the soldiers?"

"There are only some subaltern officers and the two ministers negotiating."

"Well, that's something. They should have the means to carry out negotiations with the insurrectionists." He paused. "So . . . your presence in Abidjan may not be really necessary."

But just as he said this, Baziana received another phone call.

"Speak, I'm listening," he said.

"Hello, Your Excellency?"

"What is it?"

"The insurrectionists want five hundred thousand tonight . . . Some pocket money for Christmas."

"This is absurd! What bank is open at night? What bank?" Baziana roared.

The Minister of Defense's mind went blank as he pondered the president's question. He raked his mind for what to say and almost lifelessly replied, "None, Your Excellency."

"And so? Do you want me to wake the bank manager at past ten o'clock? Is General Daku around there?"

"Da . . ." the minister said, as though trying the name on his tongue as if he was not sure who it referred to.

"General Daku!" the president said. "The general administrator of the army. Good heavens! Don't you know General Daku tonight?"

"Yes . . . Your Excellency. He's not here."

"But call him, Jesus!"

"I tried many times already. He does not answer."

"Then try Major Somi."

"It's the same, Your Excellency. They're all in the country."

"And what about the others? Have you tried Colonel Toti?"

"Sorry Your Excellency, no answer either."

"Whatever! Here is what you are going to do next. Ask the soldiers to form a delegation of five people, bring them here by helicopter. Let them leave immediately!"

Turning back to his French advisor, Baziana was so upset he could hardly look him in the face.

"If Abidjan was the Vatican," he muttered to himself, "I'd delete Christmas from the calendar. This is crazy! Can you believe this? No one, absolutely no one, works at Christmas! Getting drunk, that's all they dream about! Incredible! And they call themselves 'General'! General, my ass!"

The Frenchman had never heard him use any derogatory word before. If there was need for a sign that Baziana was depressed, this was it.

*

At the headquarters of the Socialist Party headed by François Gavana, the atmosphere was as tense as at President Baziana's. The general secretary who was in charge of the party's mass mobilization, Séverin Kalu, received a phone call that might forever change the party's destiny.

"Is this Séverin?" the caller asked.

"Hey, your voice sounds terrible," observed Séverin.

"Yes, I caught a cold, but nothing major. Everything ok as planned?"

"So far, so good!"

"Please, don't forget what François said on the phone. Are the trucks ready?"

"The trucks are ready."

"How about team A?" the caller enquired further.

"In place! I've just spoken to them. Liberians never bend, you know. These boys are born butchers Ha! ha! ha! You can say that about them – real men!"

"I hope so! Tell me, is the sergeant around?"

"Sure, but please, keep it short. We've got to keep focused."

The advisor of the Socialist leader passed his cell phone to Sergeant Bokaya.

Bokaya was truly his father's son. A champion of voodoo, he was part of the team of so-called plotters that Baziana had kicked out of the army some years back; this was after Roger Guéyo's first coup attempt. People said that Bokaya never turned his back on danger and that if he appeared to do so, it was simply to get his breath back. After his dismissal from the national army, he disappeared from Ivory Coast and was said to have returned to the secret forest where key practitioners of voodoo 'warmed up' the amulets and fetishes which Baziana's jails had over time weakened. From informal sources, Bokaya was also credited with being an initiate of the *Mashes of the Ganges*. Moreover, he was even said to have undergone the famous initiation called *The Red Pot*, a ritual of fire which was conducted in the depth of the jungle along the border of Ivory Coast and Liberia. The custodians of this ritual were originally from Liberia and were said to be descendants of the Jakuni tribe. Sergeant Bokaya and his five most faithful accomplices, a bunch of illiterate corporals who Baziana had dismissed from the army, all went back to Liberia to sharpen their occult powers for what they expected would be the final assault.

> The ferocious fire that barks
> In the abyssal depth
> Of the frostily frightened souls
>
> This sacred fire that throws
> Thousands of red lights
> Into the faces of the intrepid soldiers
>
> The soldiers with their guilty envies
> Envies sequestrated in the deep pit
> Of their souls corrupted by bitterness
>
> Brave soldiers from a foreign land
> Whose anger rhymes with their courage
> As they confront the burning firewood
>
> Brave and raging soldiers
> Over whom the incandescent pot cover
> Of the death ritual is locked
>
> Brave soldiers locked
> Under the phony heat
> Of the sacred pots
>
> Worthy soldiers whose bravery

Quenches the phony fire
Of the red pot
Only scary for the coward
But energizing for those
Who have sublime desires.

The circle formed by the masters of the initiation around the burning pots was on high alert. Inside each one Bokaya and his fearless companions were bravely battling the heat. Seen from afar, no rational mind would dare get inside the giant pots. Insatiable flames burned under each one to season the souls of soldiers for the upcoming task of seizing state power. Detractors of the ritual were adamant that the roasting flames were a mere mirage and that they only burned if the candidate in question was scared. But what was not in doubt was the courage the ritual instilled in the initiates.

After the ritual was concluded, Sergeant Bokaya and his squad exited the pots amid euphonious applause from their Liberian initiators. Their skin was exceptionally dark as if they had been burned to cinder but in reality this showed that they had been successfully anointed by the gods of fire! And so they were pronounced ready to depart for the Ivory Coast where more initiates were waiting to make the supreme sacrifice.

It was almost midnight on the 23rd of December. Gavana was still in Paris. Deep in the forest, Sergeant Bokaya stood next to his squad. Next to him was another soldier, Pierre Ambé, a lieutenant who was a close ally of Gavana's. Ambe was more serene than anyone else in the group. After ensuring that everything was in order and wishing one another good luck, they all left for Ivory Coast under cover of darkness.

*

Meanwhile, at Baziana's residential palace in Akoro, where approximately twenty republican soldiers had been assembled, the atmosphere was rather somber. Baziana mulled over the poor coordination of his private intelligence and continued to curse Christmas for his predicament. True, his trusted generals had not always been as alert as he would have liked on matters related to intelligence and his personal security. But what he faced at this moment was a complete failure on their part made worse by their seeming to have abandoned him to his fate. In addition, all his numerous courtesans had headed to the countryside leaving him alone to face the blackmail of a bunch of crazy insurrectionists. Small wonder he felt his irritation growing by the minute.

The guards at Baziana's residence, after informing him of the imminent arrival of the insurrectionists' delegation, took cover. Baziana beckoned to a servant standing nearby and ordered him to serve his favorite Scotch. However, before the servant could move, the president helped himself and poured out half a glass. The servant stood speechless. Then, after he had regained his composure, he anxiously tried to add two ice cubes to the president's glass but once again he was beaten to it – Baziana emptied the glass in one gulp and grabbed the bottle for a second helping. To be sure, he was not his usual self.

"Your Excellency," Alan Serge said, uncertain as to whether it was proper, to intervene. "Don't you think you should calm down and relax? The delegation will be here in a moment. Abidjan is only a fifteen minute helicopter ride. We should be able to resolve this problem."

Baziana, who had bowed his head, tried to open his eyes and stare at the advisor. He found it hard to believe that under the circumstances, the Frenchman could still hold himself together as though there was nothing the matter.

Alan Serge signalled to the servant to take back the trolley of spirits but Baziana shook his head firmly.

"It's unbelievable!" the president said. "They've all gone to the country . . . to party, hey? Alan?"

"Yes, Your Excellency," the Frenchman said. "But the ministers are coming with the insurrectionists and we'll sort it out ourselves."

"You . . . hic . . . you think so? So why don't we also party, Alan?" The president said. "Ev . . . everyone is at the party . . . hey, Al . . . Alan?"

"Your Excellency, I think you need to rest now."

"I am . . . hic . . . res . . . resting . . . hic. Let's par . . . party . . . hic . . . Alan."

It was not the first time that the advisor had witnessed this side of Baziana. He had on several occasions been forced to cancel scheduled meetings between the president and foreign investors because Baziana had drunk himself silly. Still, Alan Serge could not believe that, given the seriousness of the present crisis, that he could get so drunk. He swore at himself for not having been more vigilant and preventing this slide into drunken rambling. But there was now nothing to be done – Baziana's head soon drooped over his chest and he began to snore. Alan called a servant to give him a hand. The guardian of National Unity hung flabbily on their shoulders and they laid him on his super-sized, super-comfortable bed.

Once he was back in the living room, Alan Serge found Baziana's phone ringing. He answered it.

"Yes, hello."

"Mr. Devaux, what a surprise! It's Minister Akasu."

"Himself!"

"We're landing."

"Great! Not a moment too soon!"

And just as the advisor reached the passage leading to the main sitting room, the drone of a helicopter broke in.

*

Abidjan; midnight on Christmas day. The entire city had, in fact, started partying a week before, drinking, rejoicing and welcoming the holy Son of God in whom they were yet to believe. That misty night, ten trucks were driving towards their targets. They were no ordinary machines but tank trucks full of fuel. At the southern entrance of Abidjan there was a para-commando military camp. Two of the trucks parked near the camp. Those destined for the national T.V. and the radio stations and to other strategic spots in the city drove according to a well-laid plan.

The orchestrator of the plan, flanked by two other cars, drove at the end of the convoy in a huge Cherokee. The procession, to which no reveller paid any attention, moved slowly. Inside the two escorting cars were a number of well-armed men. The convoy easily penetrated the yard of the national T.V. station – the two security guards at the gate, already sore at the unfairness of being deployed on Christmas night, paid scant attention; they simply lifted up the barrier while waving at the entering cars. They had seen many such convoys and this particular one did not seem to have anything about it that could be of interest to them. The guards did not even bother about the presence of the gigantic tank trucks parked next to the national broadcasting house. Meanwhile the cars drove towards the main building of the T.V. station. Several men jumped off out of sight of the guards and began to empty fuel onto the lawn surrounding the buildings. The same procedure was repeated in all the other strategic spots around the city where the trucks had parked. If anything should go wrong with their plan, they would set these sites on fire by way of a counter-attack. The plan was really simple and easy to execute; and its implementation did not need a huge budget.

*

When the helicopter dropped the delegation of insurrectionists at the president's palatial compound, they demanded to speak to the president without any delay. Alan Serge, who received them, tried to persuade them to put off the meeting till morning. But the delegation would have none of that.

"White man," they said, "You talk too much for your own good. We are not interested in your sweet voice. And we are not interested in your sweet language either. We are here to meet the president, not you. And we want to meet him now!"

"Gentlemen," Alan said, "as I have already explained, he is having a rest."

"We are not going back unless we get our money tonight."

There was no doubt; the insurrectionists were clinging to the same demand they had communicated to the ministers. At this point Alan regretted not having asked the republican soldiers in the yard to take part in the discussion. That could have perhaps intimidated these zealous arrogant, illiterate delegates. The Frenchman could not understand where these apparently rank-less soldiers derived their determination. There were only five and none was carrying a gun. If the negotiations were to breakdown and become violent, they did not stand a chance against the republican soldiers standing outside. What was it that made them so adamant? The ministers themselves were disgusted.

"Ah," Gaston Akassu, the Minister of the National Security, said with a sigh of resignation as he mulled over the inexplicable confidence of the ignorant troopers in utter disdain.

"If not for the dialogue that Baziana has always preached, if not for the co-called democracy imposed by the West for the few peanuts they give us, what would embolden these sons of bitches, who do not even qualify to clean my swine farm, to address their betters in this manner?"

"I totally agree with you, gentlemen," Alan said, trying to adopt an assuaging tone. "But we surely have to wait until tomorrow morning. We cannot pay the money tonight, beside there is no bank or public safe in this residence and I believe you are aware of that."

"Who told you that?"

"I know it for a fact, gentlemen," the Frenchman said, finding it incredible that the insurrectionists would expect Baziana to have a public bank in his house. "I don't need to be told that."

"All is gonna be done tonight, bank or no bank" added another soldier.

"On Monday, I can promise you that. The president himself will have a word with you and . . ."

But before the Frenchman could finish, one of Baziana's servants rushed into the living room. Everyone turned towards him. One of the insurrectionists glanced at his watch. He seemed to know what this was all about.

The servant breathed in labored gasps, saying, "Sorry boss . . . you must see the T.V. There is something *inside* the T.V!"

To which the Frenchman said, "This is intolerable! Don't you see we're having a meeting?".

"No . . . boss, there's a new president inside the T.V. You got to see . . . please, boss."

The five soldiers greeted the news with shouts of delight.

"What the hell is this shit?" Mr. Akasu asked.

Then one of the delegates leaped to where the T.V. set was, and switched it on with the tip of his dirty boot.

"Hooray! Hooray!" They chanted in unison.

Good heavens! Look who is live on TV! Great Lord, if this is a mere dream, please wake us up! Colonel Major Roger Guéyo, the avenging son of the Jakuni gods, the son of the regional gods who prefer guns to agriculture and, who had been retired in the public interest, was live on all the national T.V channels.

His beret slightly tilted to his temple in a typical Che Guevara style to camouflage part of the make-up carelessly applied on his sweaty face,

Guéyo was talking. Something about him vaguely resembled a tamed adult silverback gorilla dressed up for an appearance in a circus or a provincial carnival. He was sitting in front of an immense news desk. Around him was a bunch of 'insurrectionists' who looked on somberly. To his right was Sergeant Bokaya, a sworn follower of Guéyo and lifetime enemy of Dieudonné Baziana. The sergeant had a steely look made more pronounced by his taut muscles and decidedly tight face whose brick-like, square jaws still retained the demeanor of a seasoned fighter. But all eyes were now on Guéyo who looked more like an actor cast in the role of a gangster-boss than a contending head of state who has just taken over the destinies of the country.

In his inaugural speech to the nation, Guéyo read from a piece of paper that he held nervously between his fingers. His tongue felt heavy in his mouth. From the twisted corners oozed some whitish foam that he did not bother to wipe off. Occasionally, his massive tongue rolled over his lips taking back with it some of the offending foam. The speech he delivered was faltering. From the very beginning it was riddled with gaffes.

"My dear compatriots," he began, "on this holy day of the 24th December, Baziana the dictator, Baziana the *automate* . . . sorry . . . er . . . the autocrat who lifted himself to the top of our young *demon-cracy*, pardon, *democracy* to crush it from the . . ."

It did not help that the text was hand written. Sergeant Bokaya bent over the orator's shoulder to whisper the missing word and Guéyo continued.

"Well, from the exterior. Baziana thus no longer holds the destiny of the republic of Ivory Coast. Using his policy of improvisation, he has divided the children of this nation. The fed up *popilations* have mandated our brave soldiers to take over from Baziana the tyrant and his looting friends who were leading us towards the cha . . ."

"Chaos!" Bokaya whispered rather loudly into the microphone. In fact, it appeared from his readiness to correct the orator that he was the author of the half-baked speech.

But this time, Colonel Major Roger Guéyo did not seem to agree that the combination of *c-h-a* could produce a quite unrelated sound and surely not *k*. At that very moment, the torturous thought crept into his mind that Bokaya was perhaps misleading him. After some ten silent seconds during which he pondered this proposition, Guéyo decided to proceed with the strenuous speech.

"Well," he said, " . . . who were leading us towards the *chaos*! My dear brothers and sisters, this is not a *coup d'etat*, indeed forbidden by the international *comminity*. It is in fact a *revolition* to take back . . . er, to give back the power to the people. In the days to come we will form a government of *transmission*. Meanwhile, a national curfew of three days starting from 8p.m. to 6a.m. will be observed during one week. All the *intuitions* . . . no! All the institutions of the *repiblic* are suspend . . . mmm susp . . ."

The orator was uncertain for a while. He raked his mind for the participle form of the verb "*to suspend*" for he was afraid that *suspended* would be ungrammatical. What then rose up in his head for the impassionate camera to record was decided in the heat of the moment: only an improvisation would do the trick.

"Well," he said once again. "We are going to suspend all the *institui*... pardon the *institu-tions* of the *repiblic*. Good, we call the *popilation* to be calm and keep their *severity*."

In a sudden shift of emphasis, Guéyo pointed his finger at the camera and warned:

"Now I warn you that people who have plans to stage a riposte must stop it immediately. That is correct! You can count on my words. I am not interested in the political power. I am here to clean Ivory Coast, our house".

The inspiration of the colonel seemed to have already run dry. So he turned and reverted to his scripted speech once more. But he found nothing worth reading.

"God bless Ivory Coast! Thank you very much."

He ended.

The national anthem was then sung to the relief of the viewers, concluding the endless minutes of torture.

*

After the announcement was over, Alan Serge took it upon himself to wake the president. Baziana was still intoxicated when the news was broken to him. But he was fortunate, at least in one regard, namely that Roger Guéyo did not consider his arrest to be among his top priorities, for the new head of state secretly planned to win the sympathy and support of Baziana's followers in the Democratic Party.

*

On board the helicopter, Baziana, two of his ministers, his French advisor and some republican soldiers flew towards the closest neighboring country. In spite of his fate, Baziana snored on with much abandon.

The Liberation in Question

Military dictatorship is born from the power of the gun, and so it undermines the concept of the rule of law and gives birth to a culture of might, a culture of weapons, violence and intolerance.

Benazir Bhutto

Abidjan was indescribable that night. Thieves, outlaws and maladjusted people, excited by the chaos, exploited the occasion as much as they could. There was a tacit understanding that the new regime had suspended the constitution and the rule of law. As a result, the population went crazy. Drivers were stopped and deprived of their cars; shops said to be owned by members of the Democratic Party were set ablaze; street corner stores belonging to Mauritanians were looted and demolished. Better not be a foreigner living in Abidjan that day for foreigners were said to be friends of Baziana, the deposed president, who had been facilitating their monopoly in vital sectors of the economy. These parasites had kept Ivoirians in bondage for far too long! And their importance in the informal trade sector meant that their strikes always paralyzed Abidjan. Now who had lifted them so high? Baziana, of course, through clandestine dealings! Small wonder that patriotic citizens were extremely embittered; so much so that they would stop a female passerby and rape her in the name of the revolution, of the liberation, for such a significant event needs to be properly celebrated. Stones were thrown onto the roofs of neighbors belonging to Dieudonné Baziana's ethnic group just to inform them that they were no longer in charge. Loud horns, strident whistles and throbbing drums punctuated the chaos that reigned over the city. Those who were still in the bars drank themselves silly to celebrate the ousting of Baziana. In sort, Abidjan was plundered beyond recognition.

After a few hours, a curfew was announced and armed soldiers in speedy four-wheeled vehicles started to patrol the streets. They were under strict orders to end the lawless merriment and force the population back into their houses. Soon gun shots could be heard. It was a real rout. People ran in all directions, trying to flee. It was a pity that things had come to this but they could surely continue the celebrations in the intimacy of their bedrooms. In a little while, after mounting casualties, the streets were empty; soldiers on patrol were still shooting but now mainly in the air. By morning all was quiet. One could brand it a civilian *coup d'état*, since the soldiers had only been driving brand new civilian four-wheeled vehicles. No military van or truck could be seen that night. And so the insurrectionists installed themselves as the masters of Abidjan – a fact that they intended to prove to whoever was still wandering outside in the street despite the orders.

In the up-market suburb of Cocody, as in most residential areas, supermarkets were being looted. The looters, who feared the troopers' intervention, went about their business in a great hurry. *Coup d'états* did not happen every day so one had to take the most while it was still possible. Inside the wine cellars of Cocody's supermarkets, looters ripped open box upon box of first-grade champagne. They drank, poured the priceless wine over their heads and onto the floor as if in libation to the god of *coup d'états*. Some wished they had more than one stomach to stuff in as much gratis wine as was available, but having only one miserable stomach (that they had already filled to capacity), they resorted to smashing the remaining bottles against the walls. Those who preferred clothing were no less busy making their selection. And that was only fair since Baziana and his cronies had as many suits as days in a year. Indeed, the theft of one night was like a mere drop in the ocean compared to the looting institutionalized by him and his clan. That night some of the more ambitious carried away laptops and other pricey electronics. What could be more legitimate than for the ordinary Ivoirian to also install computers in his or her bedroom as Baziana had done? One had to move with one's time. Does the future not belong to those who are computer literate?

The looters did not forget to extend their forays to the jewelry section and there helped themselves to a drawer filled with Rolexes, Baziana's favourite time piece. How insightful of them to feel that they needed to keep pace with the ex-president! In the home furniture section, far-sighted robbers worked as a team, carrying out imported bed sets, couches, sofas and armchairs. Again, who could fault them – most were sleeping on the floor of shacks and used crude hand-made stools as their dinner tables. Thus it was not really surprising that the muggers dismantled even the supermarket doors and windows.

Another noteworthy feature of this 'redistribution' campaign was that amongst the looters there was a sense of fairness and camaraderie. Anyone experiencing difficulty would not hesitate to ask for a screw driver. "I need to unscrew this door," he would announce. "My wife and kids will be proud of me tonight ..." Another would say, "Do not touch this jacket, asshole! I saw it first!" And another, "Hands off, bastard! This yellow cap is mine! I'll offer it to my girlfriend for her birthday." Or "Who's that son of a bitch who took the left foot of my pair of moccasins?" Fortunately only a few ended up quarrelling while most agreed on a fair exchange of the loot.

After the shopping centre had been stripped clean, the looters disappeared into the darkness. By the time the patrolling soldiers arrived only the last was still in view. The soldiers, who had just disembarked at the parking yard in front of the supermarkets, were enraged.

"Hey, you there!" One of the soldiers challenged as he jumped out of his Nissan Patrol vehicle. When he saw the looters hurrying off into the darkness, he sprayed them with fire, sending a dozen sprawling to the ground. Those who were not hit in the first wave of shots quickly got rid of their spoils. A couple of minutes later, the patrolling soldiers had cleared the area, leaving walls riddled with bullets, broken boxes, shoes, mattresses, utensils and all sorts of gadgets and equipment scattered over the parking yard or abandoned on the sidewalks. Along with the abandoned loot were the bullet-riddled bodies of dead civilians; some of the most overzealous insurrectionists had emptied their magazines into the looters just to make doubly sure they could not escape.

Then, once they had the stores to themselves, the soldiers went through the merchandise with a fine-tooth comb and carried away whatever they fancied. What a day it had been! Everyone left quite happy, having done their Christmas shopping without spending a penny.

*

It was six o'clock in the morning on Christmas day. The overnight curfew had just ended. Along the streets of Abidjan, huge crowds were now out celebrating the fall of the Baziana regime with the permission of the new rulers. At the main crossroads, groups of people were sitting around burning firewood in the dry cold of the looming harmattan. Many were beating drums or blowing strident whistles while others, no less joyous, were chanting:

"*Baziana, robber! Guéyo, liberator! Baziana, asshole! Guéyo, redeemer!*"

On the sidewalk some tried to enact the historic scene of Baziana's fall. Much as they had not witnessed it, their imagination did not fail them. A pot-bellied, short man wearing a worn-out jacket was holding an empty bottle of champagne. He offered to act as Baziana. When he took to the makeshift stage, he staggered as if drunk. Another held a stick representing a gun. He was the Col. Roger Guéyo of the street. He feigned to put a pair of handcuffs around 'Baziana's' wrists. "Baziana' tried to escape but 'Col. Guéyo' would not let him off the hook. This skit continued back and forth and was received by the spectators with wild applause. Indeed, people were generally joyful, celebrating the liberation whichever way their imagination permitted. Thanks to Col. Roger Guéyo and his band of fighters they were all free now: everyone would have a job; they would all have enough to eat; they would all have three meals a day as free men do. Ah, Uncle Guéyo! Thank you for being there for the people!

"*Baziana, bastard! Guéyo, bravo! Baziana, coward! Guéyo, bravo!*"

And so the celebrating crowd exchanged information regarding the previous day's events. Everywhere, people wanted to hear the latest news. And every now and then, someone would oblige.

"Silence, please! This is the latest information. Our brave soldiers have just opened the gates of Baziana's penitentiary and freed Pastor Yassa and the other democrats. There is no one left in Baziana's hell. What's more, the brave liberators have arrested some of Baziana's ministers and close friends. They'll see for themselves how wonderful life is in there!"

"Hooray! Hooray!" The joyful audience shouted back, before beginning to chant a piece that the informant had improvised.

"*Freedom lost! Freedom found! Yassa freed! Prisoners freed! Guéyo, thank you! Baziana, fuck you!*"

Somewhere farther on a spectacular convoy of cars, with a bunch of topless drunkards aboard them, entered the street. The drunkards, of course, were no less jubilant; and like the crowds on other streets, sang songs, blew their horns and beat their drums as they danced along. They were simply euphoric. In the general chaos, some wore military combat uniform and claimed to have *carte blanche* over Abidjan. They looted with abandon. It was hard to distinguish soldiers from those who spontaneously transformed themselves into militants. Storeowners and managers watched powerlessly as their properties were looted. They could not do anything for fear of provoking the wrath of the soldiers and the self-declared militants. Already, it was a favor in itself if they were spared a beating; and so did well to maintain a discreet silence – or smile as a public show of support for the liberation and not be mistaken for members of the Democratic Party.

The insurrectionists established full control over Abidjan that day. They were welcomed as messiahs. A trumpet led a brass band along the street and jubilation crowned the Christmas mood as people acted according to the dictates of their instincts. In any case, all judges were on leave, and the tribunals or courts would only re-open once the celebration was over. And once the gates of every jail in Abidjan had been thrown open, clever was he who could identify his robber afterwards. For the moment one had to fill one's attic while there was still time. After all, this was simply a present from Uncle Guéyo and his brave soldiers. In general, the new social order ushered in by the liberators seemed more than promising. Everything would be free under Uncle Guéyo's rule. No stupid taxes the Baziana way. No more roadblocks, no more prisons, no more unemployed; in a word, no more dictatorship.

Truly, Uncle Guéyo had brought freedom and authentic democracy. Already, they were finding it hard to imagine how they had endured their stifling lives under Baziana. What would have become of them if salvation had not arrived? For all they knew, they would have ended up as useless wrecks and crazy vagabonds. "Oh, Roger Guéyo!" they drowned him in unreserved adulation, "you heard our pleas, and our sorrows and you did not let us down. You chose no ordinary day to set us free. You chose Christmas. It is clearly the Lord himself who sent you! You came and bravely shouted in the face of the cowardly tyrant, 'Enough! My people have endured enough humiliation!' Oh Uncle Guéyo, we don't know how to thank you enough."

Oye , oye , oye , oye! Guéyoo, thank you! Oye , oye , oye , oye! Uncle, thank you!"

*

The following day, the National Broadcasting Corporation that was now under the control of the new government began to spread liberation propaganda. In the vicinities of shantytowns such as 'Soweto', 'Washington' and 'Zimbabwe', people began to aim their hatred at Baziana and his cabal, the cause of their misery. Armed soldiers supervised the T.V. footage; when necessary they pointed their guns at the backs of the interviewees' heads to inspire them to come up with appropriate insults against the dictator. Thanks to the liberation, troopers magically became cameramen or T.V. reporters.

The presenter of the newsreel that Christmas morning, an insurrectionist of limited education, played the journalist and read the telegrams of the nations – including France – that had decided to acknowledge the regime of Col. Roger Guéyo. In another interesting development, the political parties, the syndicates and trade unions, one after the other, came to greet, recognise and swear allegiance to the new regime. Of course, when it came to the turn of the foreign diplomats accredited to Ivory Coast, the ceremony had a more serious look.

In the main hall of the presidential palace, more than a hundred diplomats were gathered. They had come in response to the colonel's invitation to hear about the new regime. The seats in the back row of the hall were occupied by a well-trained team of zealous tribalists and professional militants, hired and ferried by buses from the most remote reaches of Guéyo's Jakuni land. The country denizens, who had never before luxuriated in the fresh blow of an air-conditioner or seen presidential luxury, came to understand how much Baziana had been screwing them. They occupied the back seats of the hall so they could clap as loudly as they pleased; the sole purpose of their presence was to endorse every pronouncement in the colonel's speech. In doing so, they would prove to the diplomats how popular the new junta was.

As soon as Colonel Roger Guéyo cleared his rusty voice, moistened his lips with his tongue and uttered his first words, a thunderous applause erupted from the back of the hall. The content of the yet-to-be-delivered speech was clearly not their business. They had been hired to clap and agree and they intended to do so with professional integrity. The orator seemed to have been taken by surprise. He was not expecting such prompt reaction from his 'faithful cattle'. He jumped instinctively from his chair and quickly sat down. This gesture did not escape the vigilance of the French ambassador (who occupied the first row among the diplomats assembled in front of the colonel). A sardonic smile played on his lips. But the enthusiasts did not seem to worry about the nervousness they had caused their master. They soon held the entire meeting to ransom, clapping as loudly as they could, and roared and chanted in a chorus amplified by a bank of microphones: *Guéyo, president! Guéyo, thank you! Guéyo, president! Guéyo, thank you!*

The colonel tried discreetly to calm the enthusiasts but it was as if he was inciting them to be noisier. The applause became unbearable. They should have stopped. But they did not. The normally unflappable Sergeant Bokaya, Guéyo's whistler, became so infuriated that, bending over the speaker's microphone, he barked at the unruly enthusiasts, "Hey, that's enough! Shut the fuck up now!"

The tone was dry and brutal like the din of a metallic bell. Since it came from Bokaya, an initiate of the Red Pot, the tough son of voodoo, the hall became quiet. The president, Col. Guéyo, looked straight into the cameras of the national and international television crews and began his speech. That day he talked as heads of state accustomed to public speeches do – without written notes in front of his eyes. It was perhaps the best way to strike back at those detractors who ridiculed him for being illiterate.

Turning his eyes from the left to the right of the huge hall, and leveling with the expectant gaze of his guests, he began, "Dear superior officers of the army of Ivory Coast, dear *sub* officers and marines and submarines . . ." Guéyo paused for a moment to assess the import of the murmur that swept across the audience. Arising from an astute instinct, he corrected himself. "Sorry, I see the *submarines* have not been invited. Anyway I want to thank our brave soldiers, particularly the *submarines*. These youngsters have been very faithful during the revolution. They are good people and we all need to recognize their sacrifice for this country. Many thanks!"

He carried on for ten more minutes before pausing to let the hired enthusiasts at the back seat of the hall do their job. But no one was prepared to clap again after Sergeant Bokaya's threat. The ensuing silence became awkward. Then Bokaya lifted up his hands like a Catholic choir conductor. The enthusiasts, reading the cue, responded at once with thunderous applause while chanting, *"Guéyo, president! Guéyo, thank you! Guéyo, president! Guéyo, thank you!"* Then he once again gave the signal and the enthusiasts abruptly ended their chants.

Guéyo carried on.

"You know, the country is not fine. Baziana was only taking care of his family business. Let me share a secret with you. This is actually a very important revelation. During the reign of Baziana, all, I say, ALL the imports of Ivory Coast were coming from one country. And so many things were brought in when they could have been produced right here in Ivory Coast. Why must we import rice from China if we can grow it here?"

He carried on while the Chinese ambassador fidgeted on his seat but luckily, the colonel, beyond the facts about the importation of their infamous rice, did not have any further interest in him or his country.

"This is, in fact, what brought poverty. The country is divided . . . the opposition is muzzled by bad laws. That's why I have request . . . hum, I requ . . . well, that's why I did request the law to be peaceful for peace is stability. Ladies and gentlemen, this country is also your country. Make yourselves at home. We are going to respect the international *treatments* . . ."

"Treaties!" Sergeant Bokaya whispered.

"Yes, yes, we are here to build our country and to do this we are going to respect international *treaties.*"

The ambassadors of France, Belgium and Canada initiated the ovation and the rest of the assembly joined in. How reassuring that the new regime had committed to maintaining international cooperation with overseas partners! The back-row enthusiasts continued with the applause long after the rest of the audience had eased off theirs. The colonel-president surprised by the stunning effect of his speech, wiped his muzzle with a piece of cloth before concluding.

"Long live the partnership between Ivory Coast and the rest of the world! Thank you. And see you again soon."

Then all the diplomats, with the exception of the Chinese ambassador who tarried a bit, rose to their feet, giving Col. Guéyo another memorable standing ovation.

*

The international airport of Abidjan was over-crowded. François Gavana and Dr Hassan Ottala were returning from France to celebrate the fall of Baziana. In the executive hall of the airport where the two leaders stood, Dr Ottala was addressing the press.

"As I mentioned weeks ago," he said, "I am back in my country, our country, to give a hand to my compatriots. We have experienced a terrible dictatorship under Baziana. Fortunately this is now part of the past. I am happy and I join my compatriots in celebrating this historic liberation."

François Gavana was equally generous in his praise.

"Many thanks to our brave soldiers for their measureless sacrifice – it has brought about this outstanding liberation. It reminds me of the Portuguese revolution and all I can say is, Free at last! Viva democracy!"

Once they were done with the press, Gavana and Ottala proceeded to meet their respective supporters who were waiting at the international airport's massive parking lot.

*

Sergeant Bokaya was no different from most members of his junta who were at best partially literate. Yet Bokaya's illiteracy did not prevent him from becoming the Colonel-President Guéyo's 'whistler'. The new president trusted him, as he trusted the other members of his junta, because such men, limited in ambition – their demands were few and mainly material – could be easily manipulated. In this regard, he was no different from the leaders of the previous regime. And so Bokaya, true to his master's estimation, was a happy man. He was happy to have found in the army of Ivory Coast under Guéyo's command (an army where no brain was required to climb the hierarchy), the only institution that could accommodate the magnitude of his illiteracy. Was it not with the new president's blessings that he had only a few years ago become a sergeant? And was he not now the right hand man of the most powerful figure in the country? For attaining such heights without any academic qualification, Sergeant Bokaya would forever be indebted to his mentor.

What a progression! From simple squaddie to presidential chief adviser! Not lacking in gratitude, Sergeant Bokaya and his men showed excessive zeal as they went about their business for their master.

In the military base of the First Battalion, newly transformed into the headquarters of the Guéyo regime, the troopers were interrogating former members of the supplanted government. These unfortunate friends of Baziana, who had not managed to escape in time, were being subjected to some uncivil treatment. Among them were the Minister of Health and the General Secretary of the deposed Democratic Party, the Minister of Industry and International Commerce, the Minister of Energy and Economic Infrastructure, the Minister of Transport, the Director of the National Revenue Service and the Director of the National Oil Refinery Company. A couple of soldiers and senior military officers were added to their number. They were being held under deplorable conditions in various rooms riddled with voracious bugs and a host of other parasites. The torture methods used to extract information from these Baziana stooges would stun the devil himself. Dressed in their underwear or in pyjamas, they lay chained on the dusty floor. The interrogators would come from time to time to question them.

That day they focused on the Director of National Revenue Service, accusing him of siphoning off money from the National Treasury that should have been used to conduct elections. Corporal Blissi, the lead investigator, was direct in his questioning.

"Where did you hide the money, mother fucker?"

The Director had a blank look on his face and did not know where to begin.

"Are you going to answer, mother fucker?"

The interrogator interpreted the director's silence as a sign of rudeness. He signalled to one of the torturers on standby to administer what they called the *iron strategy*. The man in question plugged a gadget into the wall, adjusting the button of this tool to the highest level. After ensuring that the device was ready, he prodded the sweaty back of the senior civil servant. The former Director let out a hellish cry of pain as the smell of burnt flesh filled the room.

"Where the fuck did you hide the fucken money, mother fucker? Are you going to answer me?"

Then, as he spat on the director, the interrogator, who had no previous experience in interrogation, turned to General Daku, the former

General Administrator of the army, who sat propped up against another prisoner on the rough concrete of the cell's humid floor. Daku was known to be one of Baziana's most faithful men.

"Well, let's see," Blissi said. "Perhaps the General knows where the money is . . . I am sure his magnificent mansion in the French Riviera suburb has something to do with that." And to further emphasize his point, he lifted up the former senior officer's chin with his bludgeon.

"So, my General," Corporal Blissi said, "are you also not going to say anything? Perhaps being a full general you don't fear death? Strange how our mighty General who barked endlessly, swearing to protect Baziana against one and all, even against demons, has lost his big mouth in front of the simple corporal that I am. Here is your pitiful end, dickless General."

As though on cue, the torturer prodded the General's flabby cheek with his notorious device. Like an exploding abscess, the skin on the General's cheek peeled off, exposing the raw flesh beneath. Streams of blood flowed down his cheeks, dripping onto his bare chest and continuing further down. The scalded man instinctively raised his hand to his face but Corporal Blissi's heavy boot viciously kicked the hand away, sending the general sprawling. Then the avenging corporal shouted again, "Answer, mother fucker!" However, it was as though he was appealing to a wall. General Daku remained silent. The torturers then clobbered and kicked him all over and prodded him with their electronic device. But still he did not answer. What was there to do? They left him alone for a while and Corporal Blissi turned towards Col. Sama, another loyalist.

This time he approached the colonel in an apparent show of respect and spoke to him with the cajoling tone one uses to win over a recalcitrant child.

"Please tell us Colonel, where did you hide the money? We need it so we can do our work properly and help our poor citizens who are suffering."

"What money?" the Colonel answered.

"You really don't know? Weren't you listening in on my conversation with your ministerial compatriot? Anyway, we'll soon find out. We are still searching your mansions, your castles and villages. We'll go through your mistresses' houses. We'll investigate the local banks, and your favourite ones in that Swiss paradise. All of them! Do you hear?!"

The interrogator turned round as though he was done with the colonel and then turned and struck him with his bony knee, crushing his chin. Col. Sama collapsed in a heap, cupping his broken jaw in his palms. His shrieks and groans could be heard in the next room where other captured soldiers were being interrogated. The type of torture reserved for these men was of a breathtaking severity. Some were rolled on barbed wire. Alternatively, a bunch of torturers would lay barbed wire mesh over the captives, top it with a plank and then jump on it. The unbearable bite of the barbs produced some fantastic revelations. They called this method of torture *the red steel strategy*.

Another notorious interrogation method was the *hammer-bone technique*. It consisted of striking a small hammer against various sensitive spots on the body such as the tibia, the testicles, the clavicle etc. But as successful as this was in creating co-operation, the one that delighted them most was the *warm air strategy*. As commonly used to pump up a car tire, the torturer had installed a machine equipped with a meter-long pipe that blew air into the anuses of the detainees. The unendurable dilatation of their innards would inspire victims to say whatever their torturers wanted them to say.

Now while these interrogations were going on, the crowds in the street were rejoicing. The demagogues and theorists of the revolution were waxing lyrical about the great liberation that had just occurred. They busied themselves indoctrinating and compiling for the masses new lexicons and jargons that suited their version of revolution. Knowing that most people in this country love innovation, the new politicians felt the need to coin fresh concepts that could describe the world that was about to come into being. Most of these theorists were members of the Socialist Party of François Gavana and they did not hesitate to drum up their own party slogans, doing whatever they could to gain support.

When asked to elaborate on the fate of Baziana's friends, now called 'the enemies of progress', 'saprophytes', or 'undertakers of the national economy', the crowds, in the audio-visual footages that were being shot and shown everywhere, demanded that they must be paraded naked on the streets of Abidjan then executed in the republic square; some even demanded that they be castrated and burnt alive. No one could have foreseen the speed at which these formerly peaceful people were converted into a mob baying for blood. If power comes from the sovereignty of the people, denying that sovereignty to such a people was the only way to prevent them from abusing their power. But the new military junta with *carte blanche* in Ivory Coast saw it differently. If the crowd wanted revenge, they would get precisely that.

*

It was eight o'clock, the time for the evening news on the national T.V. Since the insurrectionists overthrow of Baziana, this news edition had been the most anticipated of all. Everybody waited expectantly for the official announcement of the composition of the new government.

To say that François Gavana was stunned after the full cabinet list had been read out was a gross understatement. As per a secret agreement between the Socialist leader, the leader of the Northerners, Hassan Ottala, and the soldiers, the new transitional government was to be a melting pot of all political parties, a truly broad-based government. At the request of Col. Guéyo, Gavana and Ottala had even given the soldiers a short list of those of their members who were to be included. But the soldiers must have shredded the sheet of paper, no doubt laughing their lungs out, once the two opposition leaders had left the presidential palace. Now with the announcement, if Gavana had had any doubt about their intentions or any misapprehension as to who had taken power in Ivory Coast, these were immediately dispelled from his mind. The junta, in announcing a cabinet chart with no civilian on it, could not have made a clearer statement. But what was even worse was the calibre of these so-called 'ministers'.

"This is just incredible!" he kept repeating to himself, almost on the verge of tears.

"Absolutely unbelievable!" Séverin said, holding his chin.

"Well, well, gentlemen," Gavana replied. "As you can see for yourselves, there are no Ivorians capable of ruling this country."

"This is a betrayal, the worst treason ever," Séverin added.

The general mood was that the insurrectionists had delivered a brutally defiant provocation. How could they recruit foreigners and turn them into ministers to the disadvantage of the worthiest sons of the country? Gavana and his staff felt helpless in the face of what appeared to be the biggest absurdity of their entire political careers. Madame Sidony Gavana, who had not yet said anything, still had her eyes stuck to the T.V screen but she was as baffled as the rest of the Socialist Party bigwigs gathered in her house that evening. A myriad of ideas fluttered in her mind. However she kept her mouth shut for fear of saying something that would only aggravate the frustration that her husband and his friends felt. Still, to make the atmosphere in the room more bearable, she ventured to tackle the matter from an angle that she felt was less filled with tension.

"Why in the world," she said, "would anyone want to make that Nicolas Balafon a minister?"

"The same question I've asked myself over and over again," replied Gavana. "I cannot believe that this loony called for my help while they were writing the constitution of what is today known as the Revolutionary Rally of the Northerners."

"Nothing irritates me more than the appointment of Sambola . . . a pure Burkinabe with his fucken twisted accent. I cannot believe that such a pig now rules Ivory Coast. This is purely a provocation. We must do something about this immediately," added Séverin.

"Gentlemen," Madame Gavana said, "what if it's Hassan's hidden hand pulling all these puppets from behind the scene?"

"You have read my mind!" Gavana embraced his wife. "It's absolutely clear! There is no doubt about it. That first class analphabetic Private Toipi is none other than Hassan's former personal security officer, you remember during his prime ministerial days. Then there's this Douga, Bokaya Douga. I can't believe I gave that monkey a thousand franc note just last week. He told me he needed some cigarettes and a razor to shave his wild beard. To think that such a scavenger is now a minister!"

"The minister of what . . . how did they put it?" Séverin asked.

"Minister in charge of the Struggle against Xenophobia and Tribalism . . ." Sidony Gavana answered.

In spite of themselves, they laughed quite heartily.

"Can anyone tell me what that means?" Séverin went on again.

But no one volunteered an opinion. And with that they closed the lid on the quixotic ministry headed by the equally idiotic Bokaya.

"François," his wife said, "we've suffered too much. We can't let these buffoons steal our victory so easily. We can't allow foreigners, Burkinabe, and worse, totally illiterate people, to rule over us in our own country. They should only succeed over our dead bodies!"

"Sidony is absolutely right." Séverin said. "This is a Muslim con-
spiracy."

"I didn't say exactly that, Séverin," Madame Gavana replied.

"Not exactly your words," Séverin said. "But, you must admit that
except for Guéyo and his faithful dog Bokaya Douga, they are all Northerners and Muslims."

No one objected.

"I can't believe we were all relying on this fool Guéyo to at long last
establish real democracy in our country."

There was a glum silence. Indeed, there was nothing else to be said
– they all knew that their inaction had paved the way for Roger Guéyo's
infamous liberation.

*

On the day following the composition of the military government, the
newspapers sympathetic to the Socialist Party launched their offensive.
On its front page *The Direct* ran an article under the heading, *New Government: Foreigners Seize Power*. And in the body of the article, the author presented the genealogical tree of each of the new ministers, including that of the leader of the Northerners who was openly described as a
foreigner.

In response to this attack, since he who behaves like a sheep needs
a shepherd to guide him, the new minister in charge of 'The Struggle
against Xenophobia and Tribalism', Sergeant Bokaya, who had received
his directive from the Public Prosecutor, summoned the author of the
article and the editor of the paper. The two pressmen responded to the
minister's invitation without delay. They arrived at the minister's office
where they found a crop of enthusiastic infantrymen armed to the teeth.
In his impressive office, Sergeant Bokaya, comfortably seated behind a
massive and shining iroko wood desk, was flanked by two of his most
muscular dispatchers. His new gray striped suit – bought in haste to meet
the unforeseen ministerial functions – was too ample for his frame, and
he swam in a large collar and sleeves with endless wrinkles. It seemed
that the tailor's intention was to sew a boubou rather than a formal outfit.
As a result, Minister Bokaya looked like a scarecrow stuck in the middle

of a Malagasy rice field.

As soon as the pressmen appeared in the doorway of the said office, Bokaya dilated his broad and hairy nostrils, breathed loudly and launched into a tirade.

"You two there," he said, "If you have no proof, you are dead! Stop, right there!"

From the entrance of the massive office where the journalists stood, to the desk at which he sat, was a ten-metre space.

"What are your proofs?" the Sergeant-Minister shouted again. "Or are you just a bunch of tribalists and xenophobes! This is the last time I'm asking the question! What are your fucken proofs? God help you if you have none!"

The two men were not sure how to start their explanations. While they hesitated, the impatient Bokaya pressed a speed dial button on his telephone. The door of his office was yanked open. Before the editor could turn his neck, he was hit at the back of his head with a hammer. He dropped like a stone to the floor. The journalist, author of the article, instinctively ran towards Bokaya to escape another furiously charging soldier and reaching the desk, turned and raised his arms in surrender. But his attacker smashed an iron bar against his forehead. From his left eyebrow, a stream of blood flooded down his face as though from a faucet. After a few moments, he, too, collapsed, falling in front of Bokaya who watched impassively. After an initial silence, the minister asked his handlers not to finish off the errant journalists right there in his office but to take them away to the *camp*. Then he sent for a cleaner to wipe away the blood that had spilt on the wall and on the carpet.

The two pressmen were dragged to the basement of the building from where they were thrown into the boot of a military van. The van left the premises and made its way through the streets of Abidjan's CBD without attracting any suspicion. If Minister Bokaya's men had any regret, it was that the two journalists had died too quickly. They would have loved to demonstrate to their boss the enthusiasm for the task which he had instilled in them. Still, to have finished each with a single blow was not altogether bad and did showcase their prowess.

"Are these fuckers dead for sure?" One of the handlers asked.

"As dead as is dead," another answered. "I hit one of them myself and I know he died back there in the Boss's office."

"You can fucken kill them again if you don't think they're properly dead," yet another handler said.

"If they didn't fucken die in the office," the second handler said, "they'll sure die there in the boot."

"If they are dead, they are dead!" the third handler laughed. "And who the fuck cares? Dead here or dead at the camp, it makes no fucken difference!"

"You're damn fucken right! We just need to know where to dump these fucken bodies, that's all!"

The *camp*, really a dumping site for dead bodies, was one place that Minister-Sergeant Bokaya's men, after just one week in power, were no strangers to. So as to achieve their noble targets in the fight against tribalism and xenophobia, the junta had created the 'Court of Exception' which was staffed with military magistrates and judges who were mostly primary school dropouts. This 'exceptional court' was officially in charge of adjudicating cases of tribalism, sectarianism, corruption and all the other forms of unfairness perpetrated under the previous regime. Its main strategy was to ensure swift administration of justice; and to ensure this, the *court* even boasted a toll free number that was available twenty-four/seven.

Was your neighbor sleeping with your wife? Well, call the juridical police. In just a quarter of hour, a van loaded with a bunch of militants would pay a visit to your wife's secret lover. The soldiers would first properly tame the offender before beginning the proceedings against him. On a bad day, that is to say, if they were in a *bad* mood, one could lose one's life. The soldiers were so well organized that they had created a number of specialized units inside the military camp. If you wanted to get your debtor to pay back your money without delay or great cost, all you had to do was dial the number of the 'Black Dragon Brigade'. You did not have to hesitate to call the 'Puma Brigade' if your neighbor slandered the new government – for that was proof enough that he was against the president's ethnic group. Then in double quick time such a gossiper would be dragged before the Court of Exception to explain his 'tribalistic' and xenophobic remarks. If you felt someone had married a woman who was far more beautiful than he deserved, all you had to do was to direct your complaint to the 'Camora Brigade' which would mete out instant justice for the man who had presumed to play the part of husband to that beautiful woman. The minister in charge of the fight against tribalism dealt directly with the nation's noisy politicians and nosy journalists. The military judges wasted no time in arguments, for that to them was what light is to thieves.

For the whole of that first week, Minister Bokaya's young, over-excited militants, largely under the influence of alcohol and drugs, showed no mercy as they went rampaging around the popular neighborhoods of Abidjan. In one of them, a man said to owe a cousin two thousand francs, was slow to pay. According to a newspaper article, the creditor-cousin, who needed the money to clear some urgent domestic obligations, simply contacted the soldiers who promptly resolved the matter. The debtor-cousin lost an eye in the process. Clearly the new military government wanted to show how far it was willing to go in its fight against any conduct that reeked of fraud. After all, it was founded on a resolute promise to put an end to the impunity that had characterized Baziana's ousted regime.

*

Unlike the Ivorian masses who were still rejoicing despite the systematic decline of the economy, European expatriates, who foresaw the chaos looming ahead, were hurriedly leaving. They formed long queues along the Angoulvant Boulevard as they headed to the international airport. Their procession was as impressive as it was catastrophic. There was no peace in Abidjan anymore. The extreme brutality of the political and military tribunals did not spare them.

Very often, bored infantrymen would be released from their camps like a swarm of bees to go and recover imaginary taxes from European companies. They would stop any European even at a traffic light and interrogate him so to ascertain the origin of the wealth that enabled him to drive a brand new German motorcar while the average citizen of Ivory Coast lived in the direst misery.

"Yes, sir," the targeted man would plead. "I know most poor people can't afford supper in the shantytowns. But I honestly don't see my responsibility in such a situation."

"I agree, Mr. White Man," the soldier would say. "No doubt that it isn't your fault. I accept that. But it is surely the fault of your father or your grandfather, the colonizer!"

"I beg your pardon?"

"You French have ruined our country! Now, since you are one of their descendants, you have to carry the blame and responsibility for our poverty."

"Officer, I really struggle to locate how all that adds up. Please assist."

The hapless European, trying to reason with the intractable militant, would labor to explain his innocence with regard to the colonization of Ivory Coast. It was from sheer naiveté, if not intransigence, that these targeted individuals failed to deduce that all the soldeirs intended was to dispossess them of their brand new Peugeot 607 sports, the car *à la mode.*

"Your offence," the soldier would point out, "is that you still have not shown the receipt for your car."

"Jesus Christ!" the accosted man would say. "That's the first thing I did when you stopped me, sir. I've already shown you the vehicle's license as well as the insurance sticker, dear sir!"

"Hear me out, mister. The receipt of your car is different from the car's license and other insurance papers."

"Good heavens! Do you understand French, sir?" The accosted man would say, getting increasingly upset by the sheer, if willful, ignorance of the soldier.

Soon, the soldier, after his adrenaline level had also shot up, would run out of patience. He would cock his AK 47 and, subtlety having failed, detain his victim at gun point.

"Get the fuck out of this car right now, or you are dead meat!"

The man would open the door of his car and get out without saying a word, his hands raised in the air to indicate he did not have any desire to cause trouble. The look on his face would be that of one who has eventually come to understand that the best thing to do if you have to contend with an idiot is to yield your ground.

"Walk ahead, thief," the soldier would say. "You are a fucken colonizer and an economic criminal. Your bill will be very salty, my friend. I will teach you how bad it is to exploit the Ivorian in his own country. I am sure the colonizer does not pay his taxes. Right?"

The Frenchman would walk lifelessly, his hands clasped over his head as a sign of surrender. The soldier would escort him to the military truck that would carry him away to the soldiers' camp. Once there, they would try to determine his fiscal status after which they would slap some haphazard fine on him.

Next to the scene, another soldier would leave his peers massed on the sidewalk, and eagerly jump onto the seat of the Peugeot 607. Unable to hide his admiration, the squaddie would whistle instinctively in front of the jewel that the bravery of his colleague has in a few minutes acquired. Sometimes the militants would also act as policemen, fake a police I.D. book and patrol the streets. This was an opportunity to rape foreign prostitutes living in precarious neighborhoods.

In this regard, the story of the daily newspaper, *The Independent*, said it all: A militiaman was visiting a prostitute two days back. The man was said to have openly warned the prostitute that he was not carrying any small banknotes. Instead, he claimed to have a ten thousand franc note. The tone was so friendly, beyond any suspicion, that the prostitute allowed him to quench his burning desire. After they were done, the soldier, who, in fact, was not carrying even a cent, started to intimidate the prostitute. He threatened to have her deported since she was an illegal immigrant. But the prostitute was determined to get her pay and screamed so loudly that the entire neighborhood was alerted. A crowd quickly gathered in front of the brothel and the squaddie did not have enough time to dress before they pushed the door down. In panic, he rushed out of her room naked, his leaking tool, freshly retreated from her fetid canal, still hanging in the wind like a bell.

Never in the young history of that shantytown have people laughed that much. Fortunately for him, this laughter enabled the worthless soldier to escape through the interminable labyrinth of the shantytown's alleys. But there was a consequence: the exasperated and shameless prostitute, who had retained his pants, got his I.D. book published in the papers so that the whole city enjoyed the joke. Indeed, the squaddies were right when they promised radical change. This attitude had no matching precedent. It was clearly innovative and the results were there for all to see.

Long live woman's power, long live!

I liberate – therefore I enjoy

*The power which money bestows exceeds brute force for it purchases
the power of the bludgeon and the bayonet.*

William Cobbett

Who in Abidjan does not remember the highly publicized love affair between Marie Cathy Akossi, an ex-Miss Ivory Coast and international-
ly renowned model, and the footballer, Sekou Ba Jules, of the Monaco
Football Club, who she ended up plucking bare like a guinea fowl? Who
in Abidjan does not remember her escapades with the singer DJ Aracon
that almost led to his suicide? There can be no doubt: Marie Cathy Akossy
was a star cruncher; conning stars was her seal and trademark. As soon
as she intuited the decline of her latest lover, she disappeared. And so
no one was surprised when this applied to her 'idyll' with Jean-Claude
Baziana, the younger son of the overthrown president, Dieudonné Baziana. (Although in this case, she deserted Jean-Claude's arms because
Madame Jean-Claude had her bodyguards threaten the temptress with
death.)

But on this day she was relaxing on the silky divan of her luxurious
apartment, obtained with the proceeds generated by her sweet if corrupt
butt, and was perusing a pile of trendy French magazines. While doing
so, a quite unrelated T.V report about the launch of an HIV/AIDS campaign caught her attention. It was not that she cared so much about the
message. Rather, it was the man behind the announcement of the campaign who triggered her fancy. Normally this would not be remarkable
as she was always seeking men who had power knowing full well that a
man is always a man, weak in front of a female, and especially a female as
desirable as her. This principle has been proven true more times than she
can remember and is now her unshakeable creed. But in this case there
must be some doubt as to how successful she would be.

And so it was that, though Mary Cathy Akossi was notorious for
her capacity to pull off a thousand and one tricks, people were still surprised at how she managed to mingle with the cream of the new military
regime. They saw her ensconced among the president's delegation, seat-

ed just a row behind Col. Maj. Guéyo. Once the ceremony marking the campaign launch was over, she left with the delegation. The colonel, in person, had invited her for a *tête-à-tête* in one of Baziana's confiscated villas, and so was far from Madame Guéyo's watchful presence. After the dinner, she congratulated him on his great heart and his compassion for the poor population of 'Soweto'. She offered to organize the women of Ivory Coast into what she called the 'National Women's Squad against AIDS', as proof of her interest in community service. Guéyo was impressed by her enthusiasm and wondered how he could reward it.

"You know, my dear, I should make you the national high commissioner in charge of the fight against this scourge. You can supervise and mobilize the women of Ivory Coast. How's that?"

The ex-Miss Ivory Coast began to swing her knees in an 'opening and closing' motion without quite knocking them together. Roger Guéyo cast a furtive glance at her thighs. Affecting bashfulness, she stopped swinging her legs and put her hands on her lap as though to cover the source of temptation.

"My General," she said coyly. "Oh, pardon me, my *President* . . . forgive me, you see, I know very little about the hierarchy of the army, although soldiers of your rank have always commanded a lot of respect from me. Anyway, I wanted to say I welcome your proposal. I am overwhelmed with gratitude for your trust in me regarding this immensely important task." She suddenly stopped and swung her legs open. "But how do I thank you? I truly regret not being able to thank you sufficiently, I mean, in proportion to your . . . my General . . . sorry, my President's generosity."

Guéyo poured himself another glass of French cognac, emptied it in a single gulp and adjusted the corners of his lips to express his satisfaction. He belched loudly and tried to focus. After he had stilled himself agreeably, the president smiled, leaned towards his guest, and without diplomacy or courtesy said, "Listen, you can sleep here tonight."

"Of course, of course, my *Colo* . . ." she said, closing her knees. "Oh, this time I am *really* disgusted with myself. I can't believe that I still confuse *colonel, president* and *general.* So sorry, your Excellency. I'll try not to make that mistake again." And she smiled, opening her legs wider than before.

These mistakes by the former Miss Ivory Coast almost provoked the President-General's wrath but he restrained himself.

"You speak like some nation's ambassador whom I met yesterday. The fellow said that I deserve to be a field marshal not just a general."

The president felt at peace with himself. He slid into a more relaxed posture. Now the expert knows that when alcohol begins to get the better of most males, much of their energy is concentrated below their belts and the blood flow around that region increases considerably. Slowly, Mary Cathy began to caress the president, searching him out under his trousers. When she got him full in her hands, she began to tease and stroke him. Then, skilled performer that she was, she pulled him out and wrapped her lips around him and began to suck, first slowly and cautiously then wilder and wilder till the president's moans deepened and quickened. He held her hair from the back, trying to regulate her movements. When she felt he would not hold out much longer, she eased off and the President-General seemed relieved. She unbuckled his belt and with both hands pulled down his trousers and underwear. Guéyo desperately held onto Mary Cathy's slim hands as though afraid that she would escape.

"I am here, Your Excellency, I won't leave," she said.

But her assurance gave Roger Guéyo no certainty – if he heard it in the first place. He held her in his arms. His right hand slipped inside her skirt, groping its way down between her legs. When he found her passably wet he wasted no more time and beginning with her blouse, one after the other began to peel off her clothes. In a matter of seconds, all that remained was her G-string. It was only then that she asked the President-General whether he had any condoms.

"What?" Guéyo grunted, as though the word was unknown to him.

"Condoms. Don't you use any?"

"Con . . . what?"

"Condoms."

"Oh. Well, no. Condoms are for youngsters. It's not good for people like us."

Guéyo ripped off the G-string and parted her legs. Of course, she could not object. Then Mary Cathy guided his rock-hard manhood into her wet, warm pouch. A deep sigh escaped her parted lips. The divan shook beneath them as President Guéyo, the toughest enemy of HIV/AIDS which he swore to eradicate from Ivory Coast, rocked his lovebird as though to imprint in her mind that it was not for nothing that he aspired to become a general and the Commander-in-Chief of the Ivorian army. Suddenly, a voluptuous spasm on its way to hell traversed and shook His Excellency's body. He trembled as if caught in an epileptic attack.

"Heuuuur!" He ended up discharging after a few seconds.

What passed through each of their minds was a deep and satisfying sense of conquest.

Guéyo wiped his moustache with the back of his crusty hands, saying, "That was good, very good indeed."

"Yes, and that was only the beginning," Mary Cathy slowly replied, a tinge of sadness in her voice.

*

The following day the National Broadcasting Corporation, main mouthpiece of the junta, inaugurated the campaign against HIV/AIDS which would be carried out alongside those against xenophobia and tribalism. Guéyo himself said that these were the three most serious blights on Ivory Coast and that was his reason for creating a whole ministry in charge of this struggle.

"To hell with the economy! It's only when there is peace between citizens, and if they haven't succumbed to HIV/AIDS, that we can attend to economic matters."

The logic seemed unassailable. For how could a sick national economy provide jobs and food to households as weak as those in the shantytowns? And this logic was something only he could expound on – not that he was in a hurry to do so. But his cronies and the rest of the nation quickly embraced his programs in the hope that they would deliver some good.

So that afternoon, Roger Guéyo, who had appeared in person to launch the fight against HIV/AIDS, asked the population of 'Soweto', assembled on a crowded soccer playground in front of him, whether they had ever seen Dieudonné Baziana in their honoured neighborhood. Of course they had never seen as much as his shadow.

"Well," Guéyo said, "we want to fight AIDS together. And we want you to know that this new government likes you all. We are different from those who think that people of shantytowns are not real citizens of this country."

The crowd was touched. It was no small favor that the central political power itself had decided to come to their humble neighborhood to listen to their worries. And they praised his name, chanting, "Guéyo! Guéyo! Guéyo!"

"You, the youth," Guéyo said, "you are the future of Ivory Coast. I beg you; please protect yourselves against AIDS. Please use condoms. If not, AIDS will kill you."

And there on the podium, applauding his every word, was his new commissioner for safe sex and sexual hygiene, the famous ex-Miss Ivory Coast who knew it was not yet time to disappear.

The Northern Forces

Social justice cannot be attained by violence.
Violence kills what it intends to create.
Pope John Paul II

It was dawn when the convoy of ten 4x4 Jeeps and three AXM 10 combat tanks, raising clouds of dust, entered the village of Samo. The insurgents aboard looked mean and determined; they wielded automatic weapons, AK 47's, as well as machetes; their faces painted for war. These rebels, who had just disembarked, seemed sure of their task; they knew full well what they were looking for. Would it surprise you that they soon found the quiet, clean and modern surroundings upsetting?

In the streets of Samo the population scattered in disarray. Insurgents broke into the houses that locals had abandoned and forced out those who had not managed to flee. In this way they plundered the town and raped its women. Chaos and lawlessness terrified the local people. Some left stark naked; there was no time to get dressed for, augmenting the panic, there were gunshots in every direction. Plumes of dark smoke billowed from the roofs of burning houses. People rushed in all directions to escape the fury of the rebels. There was no time for hesitation.

Within an hour, the rebels had arrested about two hundred people, and gathered them in the public square of the little town. Encircled, the captives sat on the ground. Some women carried crying babies in their arms. A tall, robust man, who appeared to be the insurgent commander, walked to the head of the gathering. He randomly pointed his finger at a man in the crowd, demanding to know whether he was the major.

"No, boss," the man said, trembling. "I am not."

"If you are not, then who is the major?"

"I don't see him around. He . . . he is not around."

"Who are you then?"

"I am a primary school teacher. I came here from Balaké."

"Oh, really?"

The insurgent softened instantly upon learning that the man he had singled out was actually from Balaké.

"If you are from Balaké," he said, "then you are my brother, for my mother is from Koto. Do you know Koto?"

"Yes, sir," the man said. "It is ten kilometers from Balaké."

"That's right, you know the place! You are a real brother!"

The two men started chatting in Dola, the lingua franca of the Great North. The primary school teacher, who had just passed his oral examination, was allowed to leave the crowd, He walked off, relishing his new lease on life.

"Who else is from the north?" The insurgent asked. "I repeat, who else is from Balaké, Koto or Badugu? No one? Nobody else from the north? Well, well . . ." There was still silence. "In that case, guys," he concluded, "seeing there's no one, let's carry on."

He then signaled to a younger insurgent, who was about sixteen, to bring him a weapon – a large machete, with sharp double blades Pulling out of his pocket several crumpled pieces of paper with some French inscriptions, he shouted to the captives in front of him.

"Hey, you all! Look at me and listen up. I will call each of you at random. He or she will come forward and choose one of these pieces of paper. This is a lucky draw that will decide your fate."

The crowd was silent; each of the captives tried to avoid the eyes of the head of the insurgents.

"I start by you there! Come here!"

The unfortunate man dazedly made his way to the front of the crowd. Stretching out his palm to the captive, the head of the insurgents asked him to choose one of the pieces of paper in his palm.

The captive made his pick and the head of the insurgents asked him to read the inscription on the paper.

The captive hesitated, but after realizing that the head of the insurgents was becoming impatient, said, "I read 'left . . . huh . . . left hand'".

"And do you know what that means?"

"Do I know what that means? No sir, I have no idea, sir."

"Well, that means you've just allowed this boy holding the machete to amputate your left hand."

As if shocked by a bolt of electricity, the captive desperately tried to step back into the crowd but three insurgents standing nearby seized and brought him to the ground. As he tried to break free, others ran up and pinned him down. In a moment, the young boy was standing above him ready to perform his task. The captive's wife instinctively jumped out of the terrified mass to assist her man but the butt of an AK 47 knocked her to the ground. The young insurgent then brought down the machete before any other captive could interfere. The woman, who had been quickly subdued, screamed, drowning her husband's cry of agony. In spite of the soldiers grip, she continued to try and break free so she could nurse her husband but the insurgents would not let her.

"Get back there!" the commandant of the insurgents shouted. "Or you are next!"

The crowd of captives was visibly shaken; many began to weep – both for the maimed man and for themselves. They cried, imploring the insurgents to spare them. The head of the insurgents pulled out a certain tobacco like substance from his pocket, rolled it neatly in a piece of paper, and lit up. Once he had inhaled three deep puffs, he began to look at the captives with a slightly lowered forehead as though they had suddenly become hazy. He passed the substance to the young insurgent with the machete.

"Next!" he said. "You there! No, not you! The one hiding under the blanket! Come the fuck here, now!"

The man gave no indication that he had heard, or understood, much less that he was going to comply.

"Are you getting your butt here or not?" the head of the insurgents repeated. "You won't like it if you make me come for you."

The man covered with the blanket still did not show any indication of budging. The head of the insurgents, now enraged, made his way through the seated inmates, grabbed the man and dragged him to the front. With the tip of the still leaking machete, the butcher-boy lifted up the blanket and revealed a skinny man whose ribs protruded from his sides and whose dry lips were caked in sores; his temples were as deep and as sunken as his eyes were yellow; his neck and long legs seemed to be falling away from the rest of his body. Indeed, he had all the physical appearance of a dying AIDS or tuberculosis patient, yet, the man did not cough nor speak. His look could only inspire pity – but not from the boy-butcher. Over-excited by the substance he still held between his lips, he struck the naked ribs of the sickly captive, first with the flat side of his machetes, and then with the sharp edge as he hacked through the dry bones until the decrepit captive fell without a cry or any struggle.

The boy, vaguely disappointed, said, "Shit! Oh, shit! This fucker wasted my time, he was already dead!" He would have wanted to see the mutilated man writhe in pain so he felt cheated. What pleasure could one derive from defacing a man who showed no regard for pain? The boy felt so angry that he struck another blow on the dead man's forehead. Then, more or less placated, he left the body and turned towards his boss, waiting for the next instruction.

"Next!" the head of the insurgents said. "Yes, you! You over there! Drag your ass this way!"

In this manner the rebels carried on amputating the crowd. Not even babies were spared. Those in the crowd who tried to flee were luckier – they were simply shot dead. The wages of the ruling party's tribalism was the death of its followers.

*

The rebels established a new camp in Samo as a sign of their effective occupation of the small city. Then, having confirmed this conquest, they continued to progress southwards with the aim of eradicating the tribalism and nepotism that had been established by the Bando group. This they felt was the only way to bring real democracy to the new Ivory Coast. But how were they to get the country out of the present chaos that three decades of concerted effort had not sufficed to redress? How were they to heal the wounds that the campaign to eradicate tribalism was in fact worsening?

With these concerns weighing heavily in their hearts, the rebels pressed on towards Abidjan where an illiterate President was still in charge.

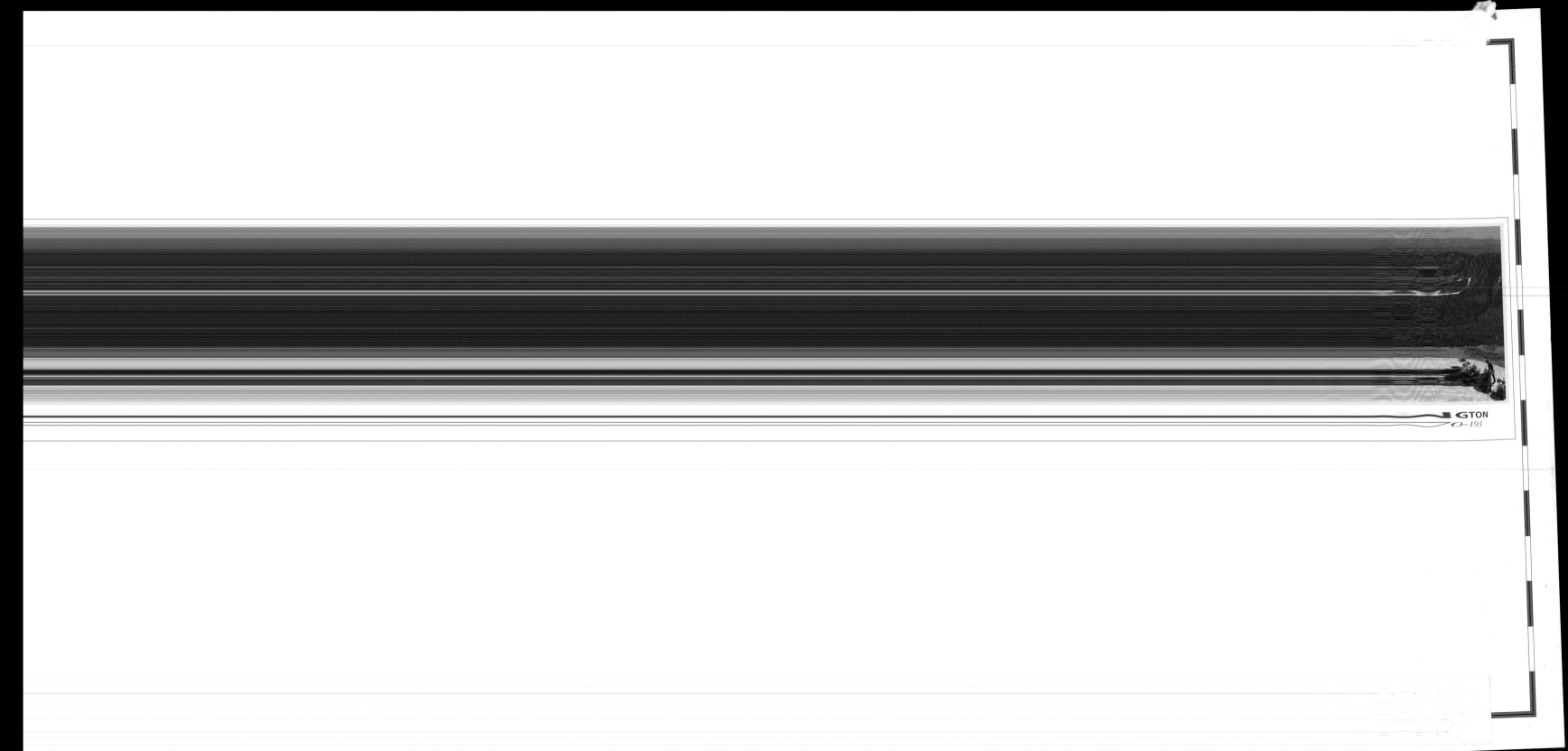

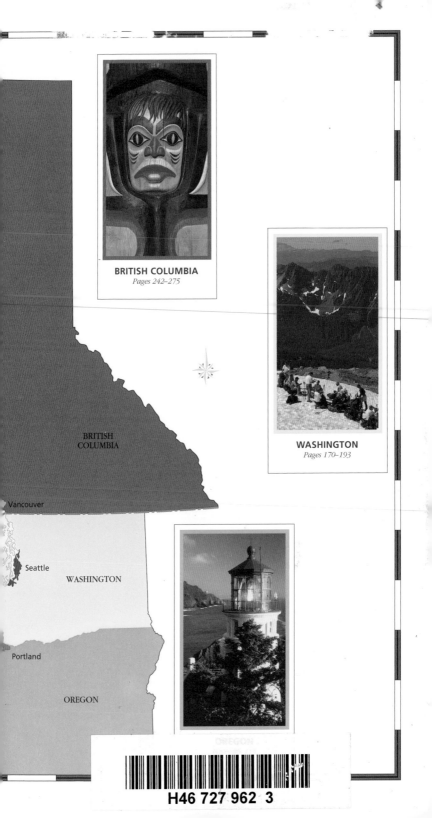

BRITISH
COLUMBIA

Vancouver

Seattle

WASHINGTON

Portland

OREGON

OREGON